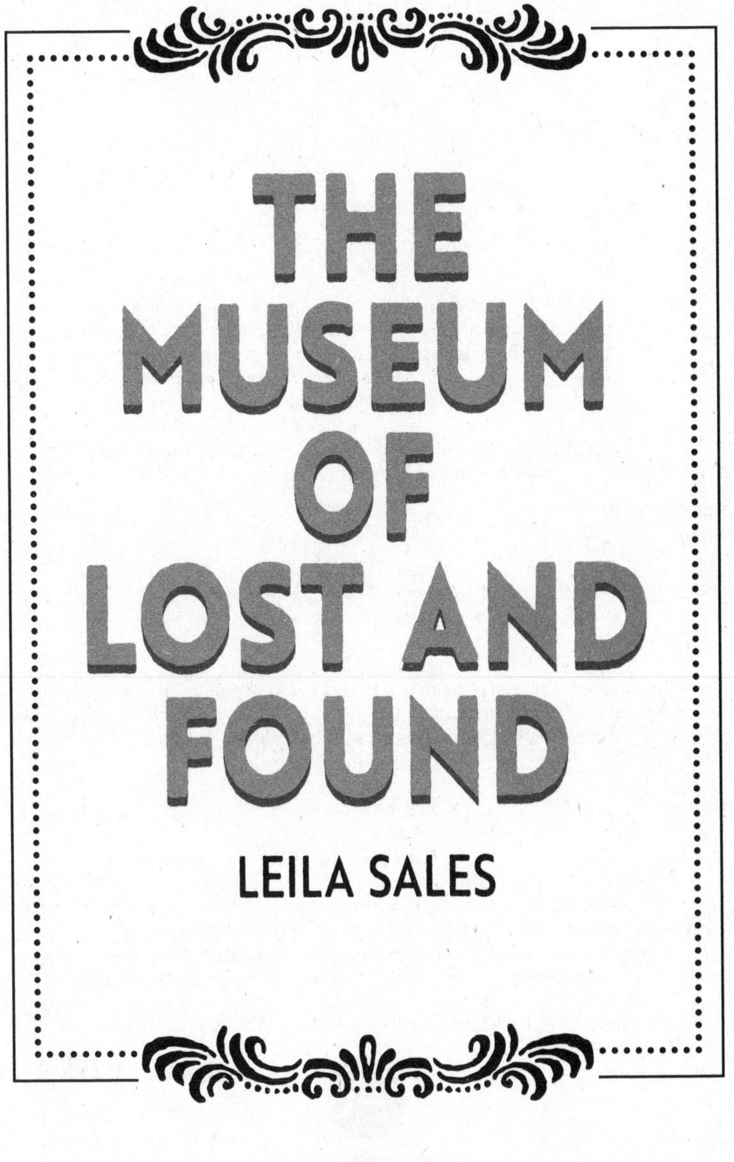

THE MUSEUM OF LOST AND FOUND

LEILA SALES

AMULET BOOKS • NEW YORK

PUBLISHER'S NOTE: This is a work of fiction. Names, characters, places, and incidents are either the product of the author's imagination or used fictitiously, and any resemblance to actual persons, living or dead, business establishments, events, or locales is entirely coincidental.

Cataloging-in-Publication Data has been applied for and may be obtained from the Library of Congress.

ISBN 978-1-4197-5451-7

Book design by Chelsea Hunter

Published in 2023 by Amulet Books, an imprint of ABRAMS.

Printed and bound in U.S.A.

10 9 8 7 6 5 4 3 2 1

ABRAMS The Art of Books
195 Broadway, New York, NY 10007
abramsbooks.com

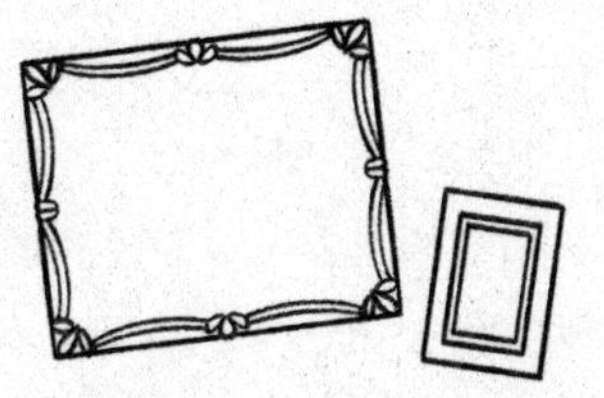

This one is dedicated to
Emily Heddleson and Rebecca Serle,
for reasons that I'm sure
they will understand

CHAPTER 1

Vanessa couldn't say for sure which happened first: finding the abandoned museum, or losing Bailey. Maybe this was because discovering the museum happened all at once; she woke up in the morning and didn't know it existed, and by the time she went to sleep that night, she did.

Losing Bailey was different. That happened over the course of days, weeks, months, so slowly that Vanessa didn't even understand what was happening until one day she looked around for Bailey and found that she was gone.

Well, that wasn't quite right. Bailey was still *there*, still a sixth grader at Edgewood Falls Middle School (just like Vanessa was), still in Mr. Howard's homeroom class (just like Vanessa was), still on school bus #12 every morning and afternoon. (Vanessa took school bus #5, but that wasn't such a huge difference.) Bailey was everywhere, except that she wasn't in Vanessa's life anymore, and Vanessa didn't know why.

There was one day when Bailey wasn't able to save a seat for Vanessa at their table in the cafeteria. And another day when Vanessa messaged her five times in a row, telling her a hilarious story about her older brother, Sterling, and while Bailey *did* ultimately message back, it took her six hours and all she said was "ha." Not even "haha," not even an emoji. One day Vanessa asked Bailey what they were doing over the weekend, and Bailey replied that she was actually going to be out of town, visiting her mean grandmother in Florida, which was fine—except that if Vanessa hadn't asked, would Bailey ever have told her?

These were all, obviously, small things. Tiny acts of negligence. Hard to prove that they were even done on purpose. They made Vanessa feel *bad*, and then they made her feel *crazy* for feeling bad, because nothing really bad had actually happened!

"If you and Bailey are having a fight," Sterling said, "you should just talk about it. You two have been friends forever, I'm sure you can work it out."

But Sterling was very stupid. Bailey hadn't been her friend *forever*, just since second grade. And they weren't *fighting*. They had fought plenty of times before, like when Bailey caught Vanessa cheating at Monopoly (only it wasn't really cheating, it was just being *strategic*), or that one time when Bailey wouldn't stop using a fake British accent no matter how much it got on Vanessa's nerves.

Fights were fine. This wasn't a fight. Sterling didn't understand anything.

Vanessa told him as much, and their mom said, "Don't call your brother stupid," and Vanessa said, "What about freedom of speech?" and then their mother sat them both down for a half-hour lecture on what "free speech" actually meant. She even brought out worksheets. It was all very boring, and Sterling said this was Vanessa's fault because Vanessa was the one who had abused her freedom of speech. And Vanessa said that it was actually *Sterling's* fault, because he was the one who'd been so stupid and wrong about this whole situation—or non-situation—with Bailey. And then their mother abandoned the educational approach and told them both to just go to their rooms and cool off.

See? *That* was a fight. Normal.

But honestly, what was Vanessa supposed to do—go up to her best friend and say, "How come your messages to

me are shorter than they used to be, and is it because you hate me now?"

Instead, Vanessa looked herself in the mirror and said, "You are overreacting, kid." That was something her mother often told her. Vanessa was a known overreactor. She was working on it.

Another thing her mother often told her was that not everything was about her. "A lot of the time, if someone is frustrated or worried or in a bad mood, they might take it out on you, but it has nothing to do with you," her mom had explained to her many times. "They're not frustrated *with* you, or worried *about* you, or in a bad mood *because* of you. You can't take everything so personally."

In other words, there could be all sorts of reasons why Bailey was being weird and distant. And many of those reasons were not Vanessa's fault.

Reassured, Vanessa went to bed, but as she was trying to fall asleep, she remembered *another* thing her mother said a lot, which was this: "Trust your instincts."

And Vanessa's instincts told her that, whatever was going on with Bailey, it had *everything* to do with Vanessa.

She didn't fall asleep for a long time after that.

Bailey's twelfth birthday was in March, four months before Vanessa's. Starting in January, Vanessa kept asking

Bailey what she wanted to do to celebrate, and Bailey kept answering that she wasn't sure yet. The previous year she'd had her party at the trampoline park, which she, Bailey, a gymnast, enjoyed immensely. Vanessa, not a gymnast, had been less fond of it. But if that's what Bailey wanted to do again this year, then of course that was what they would do.

"I just can't decide," Bailey kept saying, as the date of her birthday crept ever closer.

"If you don't make plans now," Vanessa warned her, "it'll be too late, and we won't even get to have a birthday party."

And indeed that was what wound up happening. The weekend of Bailey's birthday came and went, and they didn't do anything. Vanessa gave Bailey a card at school on Monday and said, "Are you okay?"

Bailey didn't look her in the eye when she took the card and replied, "I think I'm just too old for birthdays."

On Friday, Lisa Chang came into homeroom and asked Bailey if she'd found her scarf. "My mom's mad at me for losing it," she said.

"Oh yeah, it's in the rec room," Bailey said. "Sorry I forgot to bring it in for you today. Remind me again on Sunday."

And suddenly, Vanessa understood exactly what had happened:

Bailey *did* have a birthday party last weekend.

Bailey had a birthday party, and Vanessa wasn't invited.

She sat at her desk, paralyzed, her face burning hot.

Bailey didn't invite me to her birthday party.

She felt like she was going to throw up. She felt like she wanted to dissolve into a puddle and then evaporate into thin air and never, ever have to come back.

She told Sterling what had happened that evening as he was doing his homework in the kitchen and their mom was cooking dinner. Sterling said, "Do you want me to kick her butt? I'll gladly kick her butt for you."

"Sterling," their mother said, "what have I said about violence?" Then, as an aside: "Vanessa, stop picking your cuticles."

"I shouldn't threaten violence unless I really, truly am going to go through with it," Sterling answered promptly.

Their mother sighed. "I've said you shouldn't threaten violence, period. There's no 'unless.'"

"Dad uses violence," Sterling pointed out.

"That's different," said their mother.

"Why?" said Sterling.

Their dad was in the army. Sterling obviously knew that was different. He was just being argumentative.

"Please don't kick Bailey's butt," Vanessa requested.

"I wasn't *actually* going to," Sterling said. "She's a kid. Plus, she's a girl."

"Sterling," their mother said, "it's sexist not to kick some people's butts just because they're girls."

"So you're saying I *should* kick Bailey's butt?" Sterling asked, his forehead wrinkling.

"No!" Vanessa said.

"No," their mother sighed again. "I'm saying you shouldn't kick *anybody's* butt, not because they are girls, but because they are *people*, and violence is not a respectful way to treat *people*."

"You know what else is not a respectful way to treat people?" Vanessa said. "Not inviting them to your birthday party."

"So what are you going to do about it?" Sterling asked, and when their mother's back was to them, he mimed kicking the air, in case Vanessa didn't know what his idea for conflict resolution was.

But Vanessa didn't feel *angry* with Bailey, not exactly. Anger would be too straightforward a feeling. She felt foolish, like she should have seen this coming, like she was the wrong one for ever believing in this friendship. She felt guilty and gross, because surely she had done something to make Bailey act this way, surely there was

something wrong with *her*, but she didn't know what it was or how to fix it. She felt ashamed and confused. She felt sad and lost. This really beautiful thing was over now. This good part of her life was in the past. And no amount of crying, or begging, or wishing, or complaining, or butt-kicking would ever bring it back.

That's not to say that Vanessa didn't try. She absolutely did not accept this new reality with composure and grace. She kept trying to be friends with Bailey, because that was the only thing she knew how to be. She kept messaging her and inviting her over and referencing their years of inside jokes and wearing the earrings that Bailey had given her when they first got their ears pierced, all of this to remind Bailey how much their friendship had once meant to her. Because maybe Bailey had simply forgotten.

But nothing worked. And Vanessa could accept it or she could fight it. It didn't really matter, because either way, Bailey wasn't hers anymore.

All of this is very sad.

Let's talk about the abandoned museum, instead.

CHAPTER 2

Vanessa didn't know when the museum was constructed, but it seemed old. The building was made out of red brick and stone. It was one story around all the sides, and then had an impressive two-story rotunda in the center. There were big windows on the first floor, though all of them were broken or boarded up, and there was graffiti over the boards. A bent flagpole protruded from the roof, but no flag hung from it.

Vanessa didn't know what it had been a museum *for*, either. The only way she knew that it was a museum at all was because part of a sign remained. It said:

T E DG   D MUSE M
OF A   N   IE

She discovered the museum one unusually warm Wednesday afternoon in January. It was the sort of weather that her mother called "January thaw" and Vanessa called "global warming." She still wore her puffy winter coat, but she left it unzipped, and she didn't bother to bring her hat and mittens. Weather like this felt like an opportunity and an obligation. Everyone knew it couldn't last, so you had to appreciate it *now*, before it was gone again.

She got home from school, threw her backpack inside the mudroom, and ran outside to play one of her favorite games: EGL. EGL stood for "Explore and Get Lost," but that seemed like the sort of thing people might make fun of you for, so instead she just called it EGL because if no one knew what that meant then no one could make fun of it.

The rules of EGL were simple. You started walking from someplace you knew well, like your house. And then every time you came to a fork in the road, you chose whichever direction you were less familiar with. And you did this over and over, until eventually you had no idea where you were.

Usually it didn't take too long before Vanessa was in foreign territory. She rarely went more than mile or so from her starting point, and it was endlessly fascinating to her that there could be so many unexplored areas so

close to home. You'd think you'd need to go far away to find something new, but sometimes it was as simple as just turning left instead of right.

When you were done playing EGL, you pulled out a map and navigated back to the start. Getting back never took as long as creating the route in the first place, but it was always far more boring. Once you knew where you were going, all the fun went out of it.

Today's EGL had taken Vanessa through a park, and at the far end of the park was a cul-de-sac—which was a fancy word for *dead-end street*—and at the far end of the cul-de-sac was the museum. Large oak trees had filled in the space in front of it. The pathway to its front door was choked by grass and mud and ice. If you were not out to Explore and Get Lost, you would not have noticed it.

Vanessa approached the brick building with curiosity. If it was a museum, she wanted to go to it. Maybe. She liked some museums, like the car museum and the science museum. The art museum was kind of boring. She used to like the children's museum, but she was getting too old for it now. The last time she'd been there, she got stuck in the multistory climbing structure, which made her cry. The museum worker who coached her out kept saying encouraging things like, "Don't be scared. You

won't be stuck in there forever, I promise. We always get everyone out."

Vanessa didn't explain that her tears weren't because she was scared of being trapped, but instead because she was *different* than she used to be. All her life, she'd been able to scamper around the children's museum climbing structure with no problems, and now all of a sudden she was too big for it, and she would never be small enough again. But she let everyone think her tears were just because she was afraid—which, in a way, she sort of was.

If this museum that she'd found had once been for children, or for science or cars or art, Vanessa couldn't tell. It had clearly been shut down a long time ago. A rusty sign said, POSTED: NO TRESPASSING, and another said, DEMOLITION PENDING—but the demolition date that it listed was more than three years ago. A thick padlocked chain kept the front doors closed, but when Vanessa walked around to the side of the building, she saw that she could enter through one of the big windows, which wasn't boarded up.

So she did.

She bent over as she climbed through the window, so she wouldn't catch herself on any of the jagged bits still sticking out of the top of the window frame. Inside,

the museum was shadowy and chilly. Vanessa's boots crunched on shards of glass, as well as snow and ice and fallen leaves that had blown in.

It took her eyes a moment to adjust. Some sunlight seeped in through the windows, but that was it. Vanessa found a light switch and flicked it up and down, but nothing happened. No one was paying an electric bill for this place.

The main rotunda, the room she was in, had a high, arched ceiling, which seemed to have some sort of design painted at the top of it, though it was dirty, and from the ground Vanessa couldn't make out any details. There were four smaller rooms off the rotunda. These didn't have any windows, which meant that they didn't have so much debris blown in from outside, but meant that they were darker and creepier, too.

Vanessa walked around and saw the abandoned front desk, where guests must have once purchased tickets. The abandoned plastic stands that might have once held museum maps. The glass cases, which had once displayed items, lining the walls. Empty picture frames. Pedestals with nothing on them. Exhibits of emptiness.

It was the most fascinating nothing that Vanessa had ever seen.

She stayed in the museum until her fingers grew numb. It had been a bad choice to leave her mittens at home. And when she climbed back out through the broken window, she realized that the sun was already setting, even though it was barely five o'clock, and the temperature was falling with it. She wrapped her long brown hair around her ears and neck like a scarf and power walked home. Warm weather in January was a cruel prank.

At dinner, their mother asked what they had learned in school that day. Sterling said he'd learned dirty words to the song "Rudolph the Red-Nosed Reindeer." Vanessa said she'd learned the names for the different types of columns in ancient Greek architecture, which was true. There were no follow-up questions.

If her mom had asked specifically, "Did you explore any abandoned buildings after school today?" Vanessa would have answered her honestly. She wasn't a liar, after all. But if her mom wasn't asking, then she wasn't volunteering it. Because grown-ups . . . they saw danger everywhere. It was exhausting. What if she'd cut herself on the broken glass. What if someone had gotten mad that she was in there. What if rabid animals had made their homes in the museum. What if one of those rabid animals bit her

and she slowly died a rabid death all alone in an abandoned museum. What if other stuff that Vanessa couldn't even come up with to worry about, because even though she had a great imagination, she was much better at imagining good things than bad.

She nearly told Bailey, because she told Bailey everything. But already, even then, Bailey was being weird. Vanessa didn't know about the birthday party yet. She didn't know that they weren't going to be friends anymore. She knew only that Bailey didn't seem as interested in her as she used to be.

Having a secret, Vanessa thought, was a good way to make someone interested in you.

"I found something yesterday," she whispered to Bailey the next morning, as Mr. Howard fussed with his computer.

"What?" Bailey whispered back.

"Something really cool and secret."

"What is it?"

"You have to swear not to tell *anyone*," Vanessa said.

"Obviously."

Vanessa opened her mouth, then closed it and shook her head. "Not now," she whispered. "Find me in the bus line and I'll tell you then."

She spent the rest of the day in a state of excitement. She picked at the skin around her fingernails just to keep herself calm enough to stay in her seat. Bailey would come talk to her in the bus line at the end of the day. It would be just Bailey alone, not with Lisa or Kylie or any of the other new friends who she was spending too much time with, because Vanessa had made her promise not to tell anyone else. And Vanessa would bring Bailey in on the secret of the museum. It would be *their* secret. Theirs and nobody else's.

Probably Bailey would even want to see the museum right now, today, although it had gotten cold again overnight and was not an EGL sort of day. Bailey would get on Vanessa's bus so they could go explore the museum immediately. Hopefully she'd even stay for dinner.

The museum was cool, but mostly it was a means to an end, and that end was Bailey. Vanessa was glad she'd found it.

But the school day ended, and none of that happened. Vanessa waited and waited until she was the last one to board her bus, and still Bailey hadn't come to talk to her. Vanessa caught sight of her out the window as the bus pulled away, laughing with some of her new friends in the #12 bus line.

Vanessa had a secret, and Bailey didn't care, didn't remember, or both.

Vanessa turned her face away from the window and curled her knees up to her chest. This was the problem with imagining good things.

CHAPTER 3

The more Bailey disappeared, the more often Vanessa went to the museum. By March, as the buds began to appear on the trees and the sun set later and later, Vanessa was checking on the museum most days after school, whenever she didn't have to spend her entire afternoon at Hebrew school or at a playdate. Sometimes she had playdates. She had other friends. It's just that none of them were Bailey.

The weekend after the Birthday Party Incident, Vanessa decided that if she was going to basically be using the museum as her personal secret hideout, she needed to clean it up a little.

"Do we have a broom?" Vanessa asked Sterling.

"Of course," he said. "What kind of house doesn't have a broom?" He was reading a book on the living room couch.

"Where is it?"

"I dunno." Sterling turned the page.

"I can't believe you two," their mother said, coming in from the kitchen. Vanessa hadn't known she'd been listening. "You've lived here for, what, five years? And you don't even know where we keep the broom?"

"Why would we know where the broom is?" Sterling said.

"Because maybe you've swept a floor? *Ever?*"

"I'd sweep a floor if it was dirty," Sterling volunteered. "Our floors are never dirty."

"Right," their mother said. "Because I always sweep them."

"So where's the broom?" Vanessa asked again.

Her mother got it out for her. It was hanging on the back of the basement door.

"Well, of course I didn't know where it was," Vanessa said. "I'd have to go down into the basement to get it."

"You wouldn't have to go *into* the basement," her mother said. "You'd just have to open the door to the basement. You could reach around and grab the broom without even looking."

"You know I don't go into the basement," Vanessa said. "There might be spiders down there."

"Oh, there are *definitely* spiders down there," Sterling said. "Tons of them."

"You see?" Vanessa said to her mother.

"Spiders are good," her mother said. "They eat mosquitoes."

"They're creepy," Vanessa said. "I don't trust anyone with more than four legs." She took the broom from her mother and headed out of the living room. "Thanks," she called over her shoulder.

"Are you actually going to sweep the house?" her mother asked, like she couldn't believe her eyes.

"What?" Vanessa asked. "No."

She grabbed a box of garbage bags from under the kitchen sink and went outside. "Don't play any pinball today," her mom called after her.

"Okay," Vanessa yelled back, closing the back door tightly behind her. "I won't."

She headed to the museum, stepping around the last melting piles of slush. She imagined what people in the passing cars might think she was up to, if they saw her walking down the sidewalk with a broom. Maybe they would think she was a scullery maid. Or maybe they

thought she was a secret wizard and she was using the broom for Quidditch practice.

Vanessa's mother had explained to her and Sterling a concept called "Occam's Razor." It meant that the simplest explanation was usually the correct one. Vanessa had no idea why it was called that. Who was Occam? What did a razor have to do with anything? Was it a shaving razor, like her dad used, or a Razor scooter, like Bailey had? What was the Occam's Razor explanation for the name Occam's Razor?

Anyway, Vanessa thought that the simplest explanation for an eleven-year-old walking down the sidewalk carrying a broom would be that she was a secret wizard, but in this case, the simplest explanation was wrong. Take that, Occam.

She climbed in the broken window to the museum and got to work. She swept out the dried leaves, the dirt, the shards of glass. She even swept out a couple of spiderwebs, which she felt was very brave of her. "Good job, Vanessa," she said, because there was no one else there to say it to her. "Great work overcoming your fears."

Interacting with spiders was not ideal under any circumstances, but here at the museum it felt like a necessity. If Vanessa didn't handle these spiders, nobody else

would. Unlike the spiders in the basement at home, which could always be somebody else's problem.

The whole museum felt like that: like she was the only one who cared. She was the only one who even knew it existed. In that way, it was the only place in the world that felt like it truly belonged to her. Even her own home was technically her mother's home. There were all these rules and systems, like that coats had to get hung up in the front-hall closet as soon as you took them off, and that wet umbrellas had to be left in the mud room, and that fruits went in the left-hand drawer in the refrigerator while vegetables went in the right-hand drawer, except for tomatoes which didn't go in the fridge at all.

And honestly Vanessa didn't *object* to any of these rules—except for the one about hanging up your coat right away, which was inconvenient, because sometimes she just needed to go to the bathroom and eat a snack and then she was going to head right back outside, so it was a huge waste of time to hang up her coat for all of ten minutes and then take it back out of the closet. But even when the rules were fine, they certainly weren't choices that she had made, or anything that she found important.

At school, too, nothing felt like it one hundred percent belonged to her. Not even her own belongings. Mr. Howard

would sometimes do unannounced inspections where he'd have everyone in the class open up their backpacks, and if all their pens and folders and notebooks weren't arranged the way he thought they should be, he would give them a check minus for "organization." And while "organization" wasn't a real subject—it wasn't *math*—Vanessa didn't like getting check minuses in anything, so even her own books were the way that someone else wanted them.

The museum felt like the only place where she was entirely responsible and entirely in charge.

So that was why she was the one sweeping it now, piling up bag after bag of debris. She found random stuff, like empty McDonald's fry containers and a tennis ball that looked like a dog had chewed it up. She could see dust mites in the beams of light, and they made her sneeze. Sweeping was hard work—before long, she'd developed a cramp in her left side, and she wasn't coordinated enough to switch to her right. But it was rewarding, too. She liked seeing her pile of trash grow bigger and bigger. She liked being able to see exactly what she was accomplishing.

She kept a battery-powered lantern at the museum now, which she'd gotten for the single Girl Scout camping trip she and Bailey went on, before they decided they didn't want to be Girl Scouts. It had just been sitting in the back

of the coat closet since then, so Vanessa knew her mom wouldn't notice that it was gone. She turned it on now so she could thoroughly inspect the four windowless side rooms. The first three all had litter in them—some broken display cases and crumbled-up newspapers, a bent spoon, and a cracked coffee pot. Stuff that had maybe once been museum exhibits, or that maybe had just found its way here: a hat, a rope, a wooden chair, an encyclopedia.

But in the fourth room, Vanessa found something different: a large framed canvas. It was a painting, though the painted side was leaning against the wall, so she couldn't tell what it depicted.

Vanessa took a deep breath, reached out her hands, and yanked the painting toward her. Then she screamed. Had a bunch of spiders been hiding between the canvas and the wall and were they now skittering away? Probably. She thought she felt something brush against her ankle, and she screamed again for good measure.

She dragged the painting out into the main room with her as fast as she could—which was not fast enough, because it was quite heavy and wider than she was tall. At least in the main room, with its big windows, if spiders went on the attack, she'd be able to see them coming.

She leaned the painting against a wall and stepped back to look at it.

It was beautiful. It showed a wide, dewy green field with trees. A sturdy marble plinth sat in the center. Carved into the marble was an angelic face. A stream of water poured out of the face's open mouth and pooled into the small trough below. It looked almost realistic, like a photograph, only everything was enhanced: the water sparklier than it would be in real life, the grass greener.

There were two figures in the painting: both girls, both around the same height as the plinth. One wore her curly hair in an Afro. She had on high-waisted bell-bottom jeans and a cropped shirt. The other had long, straight hair and was dressed in a boxy orange dress with lots of bangles on her arms. They were laying out a picnic before them: a gingham blanket, a wicker basket, a loaf of bread, a wedge of cheese, a bottle of soda.

Vanessa felt like it could have been a painting of her and Bailey. The two figures in the painting didn't *look* anything like she and Bailey did. (For one thing, neither Vanessa nor Bailey wore very much orange.) But the togetherness of them. This moment they were sharing. Vanessa recognized it, deep inside her soul.

Vanessa wanted to step inside the painting and live there, in this world of closeness. But of course that was impossible. So instead, for a moment, she just took it in. She imagined it hanging on one of the museum's once-bright walls, visitors coming from all over to see it just as she herself was doing now. How long ago must that have been?

"I'm here now," she told the painting. "I'll make this place good for you again."

When she didn't have the energy to clean anymore, Vanessa climbed on top of the ticketing booth so she could survey all that she'd done. It looked better. It definitely looked better. She nodded her head, jumped off the counter, and took the broom back home.

She felt pleased with herself all through dinner and homework and screen time, but then when she was alone in bed, trying to fall asleep, it occurred to her to feel bad again. That was the thing about sadness: You could cover over it really well, but sometimes it just came back, without any warning. Sometimes Vanessa didn't even immediately remember *why* she was feeling bad, and then she'd sort of poke around her mind for the cause—like having a cavity and prodding at all your teeth with your tongue until one of them gives you a flash of pain.

That's what Vanessa did as she lay in bed. *What's making me feel this way? Is it Mom? Is it the museum? Is it school? Is it Bailey? Ah, yes, there we go. There's the pain. I found it, hiding right where it's supposed to be.*

She climbed out of bed and unpinned a sheet of paper from her bulletin board. She could only sort of read it in the moonlight, but she already knew what it said: *This hereby certifies that Vanessa Lepp and Bailey Dominguez are officially best friends and promise to uphold the Best Friend Code forever.*

They'd both signed the certificate. Vanessa had been stupid enough to believe they both meant it. She hadn't realized that forever could be so short.

She put it facedown on her desk and buried it under a bunch of books, where she would no longer have to see it every morning and every night, reminded each time of broken promises.

CHAPTER 4

The next Sunday, Vanessa's Hebrew school class went on a field trip to the Jewish Museum downtown. It was a whole production. It took a million years to load everyone onto the school bus, and once they were all onboard, it took another million years to leave the parking lot because Ms. Adler somehow could *not* get an accurate count of how many kids there were. She walked up and down the aisle, muttering numbers to herself, and sometimes she counted 21 and once she counted 19, but either way she kept not getting 20, which was how many kids were *supposed* to be on the bus. *"Shechet!"* Ms. Adler shouted over and over, which was Hebrew for *quiet!* And *"Shechet b'vakasha!"* which meant *quiet, please!* As though the problem was that her students were talking and not that she, Ms. Adler, was just very bad at counting by twos.

It didn't help matters that all 20 (or 19, or 21) of them were wearing the same shirt, which was neon green and said TEMPLE BETH ELOHIM on the front, with the temple's phone number on the back. This was supposed to be so they wouldn't get lost on their field trip, or at least if they *did* get lost, anyone who found them would know to return them to Temple Beth Elohim. Sort of like Sharpieing your initials on your toys. The shirts seemed unnecessary to Vanessa, because if she got separated from everyone else, she was fully capable of just opening her mouth and saying, "Call my mother, Miranda Lepp, at the following phone number, please and thank you."

Vanessa's primary objection to the matching shirts was not that they were unnecessary (even though, again, *they were*), but rather that they drew too much attention to who was and was not naturally cute. Vanessa knew that she was not: her hair was too bushy and tangly, and she had a scar on her upper lip from the cleft lip surgery she'd had as a baby. When she wore a cute outfit, she felt like people looked at that more than they looked at her face. But when she wore the same thing as everyone else, she felt like she

was in some weird magazine-style competition of "who wore it best?" and the answer was never her.

Bailey was naturally cute, and so were a lot of Bailey's new friends, like Lisa and Kylie. Most of the time, Vanessa didn't think that Bailey had chosen other people over her just because they were cuter. Only an incredibly dumb, superficial person would pick friends based on cuteness, and Bailey was neither dumb nor superficial.

But then she sometimes thought that maybe if she were cuter she *would* win Bailey back, somehow. Like maybe it was harder to abandon an extremely cute person. Bailey had never said anything like "I don't want to be your friend anymore because your hair is bushy," but then Bailey had never given one single reason why she didn't want to be Vanessa's friend anymore, so all Vanessa could do was guess.

The Jewish Museum was very different from Vanessa's museum. It was large, clean, and new, with angular walls and modern art. Each room or wing was dedicated to a different topic. In the first wing, which was called "Jewish Artifacts," they were greeted by a peppy, curly-haired woman named Michele. Michele told them that she was one of the museum's curators. "Does anybody know what a curator is?" she asked.

Vanessa did not.

"*Curators* are people who put together museum collections," Michele explained. "We decide what exhibitions to show, which items should be on display, and how they should be presented."

Vanessa wondered if curators were also bad readers. Michele definitely seemed like she had not read the words on the front of their T-shirts—every one of which, again, said TEMPLE BETH ELOHIM in a huge font—because she started talking to them like they were a bunch of random kids off the street who had never heard of Judaism before, not like they were a Hebrew school class of students one year away from their bar and bat mitzvahs.

"Does anyone know what *this* is called?" she asked them, pointing at a large scroll behind glass.

"A Torah," all the kids muttered. They'd covered this in like Hebrew school pre-K.

"Amazing!" Michele cheered. "And does anyone know what the Torah is for?"

Becky Felsenstein's hand shot up into the air. Becky loved answering questions. Vanessa liked answering *some* questions, but only the interesting ones.

"It's the most important book in Judaism," Becky said breathlessly. "The Torah tells the story of the Jewish people, and it's thousands and thousands of years old."

"Great job!" said Michele.

They kept doing this around the Jewish Artifacts exhibition, and Michele kept acting like they were geniuses for knowing anything. Vanessa thought that she just had very low expectations for them. None of them were like religious *experts*; they were just normal kids who had grown up in Jewish homes, so they'd always been around these things. It would be like if there was a museum displaying bathroom sinks and teakettles. *What do you think these are for?*

It struck Vanessa as odd, seeing examples of all these objects that they used and touched and ignored on an everyday basis, but here at this museum those same objects were behind glass, on display, with placards beside them explaining their purpose. Like, Vanessa's family's menorah—the candelabra that they used to celebrate Hanukkah each winter—had some gummy candle wax stuck to it that they could never fully peel off. One of its ceramic candle holders was chipped. But *this* menorah was clean and perfect and preserved. It showed what a menorah looked like, but it also seemed like it never got used for the purposes of being a menorah.

It was weird to see parts of your life on display, as though they were history.

"This is called a *yad*," Michele said, gesturing toward a pointer whose tip was shaped like a small hand. "Does anyone know what it's used for?"

It was used for reading the Torah, but Eli Schaefer spoke up then and said, "It's for picking your nose."

The rest of the students giggled, so Vanessa did, too.

"Excuse me?" Michele's smile slipped slightly.

"Yeah," Eli went on. "It's an ancient nose-picking device. You ever get a big booger stuck up there, but your finger just can't *quite* reach it? That's when you bring out the yad and just ram it all the way up your nostril. *Bam!*" He mimed the action.

Eli was the class clown. This wasn't Vanessa's opinion—it was his entire identity. He literally wore a T-shirt that said CLASS CLOWN on it. Not all the time, of course—today he was wearing the same shirt as everybody else—but sometimes. Enough so you didn't forget that he was funny.

Michele looked confused. Ms. Adler clapped her hands once and said, "I think that's enough Jewish Artifacts for now. Let's move on to the next room, shall we?"

The next room was much more interesting. It was a temporary art exhibition featuring paintings and drawings by famous Jewish children's book illustrators, like Maurice

Sendak and Simms Taback and Shel Silverstein. Vanessa had grown up with copies of some of their books, but she'd never seen the original artwork before—the actual pieces of paper that these famous people's hands had actually touched. It made her think about the big painting she'd found in the side room at the museum. A real artist had touched that canvas.

She wished that Bailey were here, because Bailey loved books and she'd be impressed. But Bailey wasn't Jewish, so she didn't go to Hebrew school.

"Has anyone heard of any of these illustrators before?" Michele asked.

"I know Maurice Sendak," Eli volunteered. "He's the guy who wrote that book about the naked kid, where you can see his you-know-what."

Eli was really on a roll today.

"These pictures don't show any Jewish stuff," Vanessa said. "So how come they're in the Jewish Museum?"

"Because the artists are Jewish!" Becky blurted out, thrilled to have such an easy-to-answer question.

"Yeah, I know that already," Vanessa said with a frown. It just didn't seem like that should be *enough*. They were Jewish, and they made art, so therefore it was Jewish art?

Was it that simple? If her mom made tacos, would they automatically be Jewish tacos?

"That's a good question," Michele told Vanessa, who resisted the urge to stick out her tongue at Becky and say *take that.* "It's the curator's job to decide what type of exhibitions belong in the museum and what types of items belong in each exhibition. As a curator, I think about what the point of the museum is—what we want visitors to take away—and all the different ways that we can get that point across. Other curators might argue that this exhibition *doesn't* belong in this museum, but I think it does because it displays some of the contributions that the Jewish people have made to arts and literature."

The final room they visited was called the Remembrance Room. It was filled with historical information about Jews who'd been persecuted and killed for their religion. In the display cases were old passports, Stars of David, and black-and-white photographs. There was a falling-apart pair of boots that a Jewish girl had worn when she was fleeing the Nazis. "Looks like someone could've used a shoeshine!" Eli joked.

"Hey, Eli?" Ms. Adler said. "Knock it off. People died."

Eli kept quiet after that.

Sometimes Vanessa wished she could think of as many jokes as Eli. Other times, she was glad that she couldn't.

Lots of the items in this room came from Germany and nearby countries that the Nazis had invaded. Germany was where Vanessa's dad was stationed now. It was so different these days, though, her dad said. Eighty years had passed since World War II, and the world had changed. There wasn't a Nazi party in Germany anymore. They'd taken all sorts of steps to make sure that the Holocaust could never happen again.

Still, Vanessa's mom was weird about Germany. They'd spent last summer there, staying near Dad's base, and Mom had flinched every time a voice came on the loudspeaker at a train station to say *"Achtung!"*—German for "Attention!" Vanessa's great-great-grandmother had been killed in a Nazi concentration camp, long before Mom was even born.

As the class was herded out of the Remembrance Room, Vanessa wondered whether her great-great-grandmother's shoes or passport or photographs were in a museum somewhere, if some other girl was looking at them on a field trip right now.

Probably not. Most things never wound up in museums. Even if they should.

They all got back on the bus, and Ms. Adler counted them again, even though of course nobody had gone missing. Eli was in the seat across from Vanessa, and he spent the whole ride home miming picking his nose with a yad, much to the delight of the class.

You laugh at people who pick at their bodies. Everybody knows this.

Vanessa tuned out the laughter. Because she had an idea. A really good, really *big* idea.

Instead of using her museum as a secret hideout, she could return it to its actual purpose. She could make it be a museum again. It could display artifacts and art and history, with labels and explanations.

But it wouldn't be a museum about Judaism, because that museum already existed. And anyway, Vanessa didn't have enough Jewish items or knowledge to have any business starting a museum like that. *Her* museum would be about something where she had tons and tons of objects and information. It would be about something where she was the expert.

It would be the museum of Bailey.

And maybe by telling the story of Bailey—by laying it all out clearly behind glass—she would at last be able to understand where it went wrong.

CHAPTER 5

The next week, Vanessa began the process of moving her Bailey belongings into the museum. The best friend certificate that she'd pulled off her bulletin board was only the start. She found stuff that reminded her of Bailey in her room, her locker, all over the house. It was everywhere. She put each item in her backpack, sometimes inside a plastic bag to keep it clean, and carried it to the museum. There, she placed each item inside a display case. She carefully stuck a number next to it, and she wrote up a description to hang on the wall beside it.

ITEM #5: FRAGMENT OF A FRIENDSHIP BRACELET

Materials: embroidery thread.
Bailey stitched this bracelet for me over spring break of fourth grade. I had to visit my dad in Virginia, so we didn't see each other for the whole week. I wore it every day for almost a year after that until the knot unraveled.

ITEM #8: THE DAYS ARE JUST PACKED: A CALVIN AND HOBBES COLLECTION, BY BILL WATTERSON

Materials: paper.
This book used to be my mom's, but Bailey and I read it so often that now it's ours. It's our favorite comic book. It's about a boy named Calvin and his pet tiger,

Hobbes. Other people think Hobbes is just a stuffed animal, but Calvin knows he's real. They're best friends who always get into trouble together, just like Bailey and me—that's why we liked them so much. Sometimes in the comic, Calvin's mom or teacher gets mad at them, but Calvin and Hobbes always stick together.

ITEM #12: SHH!: VOL. I, ISSUE I

Materials: paper.

SHH! was a gossip magazine that Bailey and I started last year. It was going to be like US WEEKLY or STAR or one of those other magazines at the front of the

supermarket checkout line, where they tell you how Princess Kate is pregnant with triplets and the real reason why Brad and Jen broke up, even though no one knows or cares who Brad and Jen are. The difference is that SHH! was going to be filled with gossip about kids in our school.

We did tons of investigative reporting and wrote some really searing news stories. But we only got out one issue before Keiko Cho's mom complained to the principal and he shut it down. Mrs. Cho objected to the article about how Keiko faked a peanut allergy just so she could be in Mr. Van Stampfel's class. Even though it was TRUE, Keiko DID fake a peanut allergy so she could be in Mr. Van Stampfel's class, and like all good reporters we were simply stating THE FACTS, but we had to stop making SHH! anyway.

"Where are you going all the time?" Sterling asked Vanessa on Thursday afternoon. She had her backpack full of Bailey objects slung over her shoulder, and was about to walk to the museum.

"What do you mean?" Vanessa asked, pausing in the doorway.

"You keep coming home from school and immediately going out again, even when it's raining, and not coming back until Mom's home from work."

"So?" Vanessa challenged him.

"So, where are you going? I know you're not going over to Bailey's anymore."

"I have other friends," Vanessa said.

"Like who?"

"Rosalie and Honore, to start."

Vanessa liked Rosalie a lot. She liked Honore less. But that didn't really matter, since they came as a package deal.

"And are you going to hang out with Rosalie and Honore?" Sterling asked.

"Why are you even paying so much attention to what I do after school, anyway?" Vanessa asked. "I don't care what *you* do every day."

"I know you don't," said Sterling.

"What are you, like, *obsessed* with me?" Vanessa said. "Just because you never go anywhere or do anything doesn't mean that I shouldn't."

"Forget it. Do what you want. Just make sure you're home in time for Dad's call."

"I know," Vanessa said, but Sterling had already started reading his math textbook and didn't seem to be listening

anymore. Vanessa pulled on the other strap of her backpack and walked out.

When she got to the museum, she did a pass around all the displays, to make sure everything was looking good. A label had fallen down, so Vanessa taped it back up. She needed to sweep again—new leaves and debris had blown in through the broken window. Sweeping was so dumb. Every time you did it, it lasted for hours or a day or a few days, but inevitably at some point you just had to do it again. Why couldn't anything just stay swept?

If she could seal up the window, then junk from outside wouldn't get in so easily. But the broken window was her only entrance, so she couldn't board it up completely. Vanessa settled for hanging a garbage bag from the window, like a curtain. She could still push through it, but hopefully some of the litter couldn't.

She unpacked her bag and started setting up the new exhibits, which ultimately led to rearranging some of the pieces that were already on display. Up until now, Vanessa had been putting items out randomly, wherever they fit. But now she was thinking they needed some kind of order to them.

She could organize it chronologically, with the items from when they were little kids placed first, and the most

recent memories coming at the end. If she did that, then the first display would be her Gibby Giraffe stuffed animal.

Gibby Giraffe was a lesser-known cartoon character whom Vanessa used to adore. She had insisted on bringing her Gibby Giraffe to the first day of second grade, even though Sterling had made fun of her. He'd said that she was too old for a stuffed animal, and that Gibby smelled bad. (Gibby did not smell *bad*. She just smelled . . . well loved.) When Bailey saw Vanessa holding Gibby, she gasped and ran right up to her and said, "Gibby Giraffe is my favorite, too! My name's Bailey. Let's be friends!"

The moral of the story was that Sterling was wrong, as usual, and that you should always be up-front about stuff that you liked, because that was how you found other people who liked it, too.

On the other hand, maybe Vanessa *shouldn't* arrange the museum in chronological order. Maybe she should organize it by theme. She could do a section of letters and postcards from Bailey. A section of artwork they had created together. A section of presents Bailey had given her. A section of photos.

But then it was hard to know which section some items belonged in. Bailey's favorite place mat, the one with pictures of guinea pigs, which was always at her place when

she came over for dinner—that seemed like it was in a category of its own. And a piece of pottery that Bailey had made and given to Vanessa as a Hanukkah present could go in either artwork *or* presents, and how could she choose?

The point was to tell their story the right way. To make it so clear that, if Bailey came to see the museum, she couldn't help but understand that their friendship was perfect, it was magic, it was everything. If Bailey visited the museum, she would remember what they'd had. She would want it back.

Vanessa worked for a while longer, then checked the time. Her dad would be calling soon, and she didn't want to miss it. Because of the time difference and his work schedule and her school schedule, it could be a while before they were available at the same time again. They texted every

day, but that wasn't the same. "I have to go," she told her museum. "I'll be back tomorrow. Don't go anywhere."

This was a joke, of course. Unlike the real Bailey, the museum of Bailey couldn't go anywhere or be anything other than what Vanessa made it into.

She climbed through the window, jogged home with her now-empty backpack, and scooted in the front door just as the family iPad was ringing. "Me, me, me!" she shouted, but Sterling was already picking it up. He stuck out his tongue at her, and popped in headphones so she couldn't eavesdrop on what their father was saying.

"Hey, Dad," he said. "How's it going? . . . Cool, yeah, me too . . . You psyched for opening day? Adams has been looking pretty good in training . . . I'm serious . . . I know, it's gonna take us a while to rebuild after—Yeah, trading away Jose was the stupidest thing they've ever done, but give Adams a shot, he has potential . . ."

Vanessa rolled her eyes and went into the kitchen. She opened the fridge. She did it as quietly as possible, but somehow her mom still heard.

"What are you looking for?" her mother asked, immediately coming into the kitchen.

"A snack."

"I'm going to start dinner in just a few minutes."

"I know," Vanessa said. "But I'm hungry now." She hadn't taken the time to eat anything between school and the museum, and now it had caught up to her all of a sudden. Vanessa was terrible at predicting when she was going to be hungry. It wasn't something that happened to her little by little. She'd be totally fine, food the last thing on her mind, and then *bam!* she'd suddenly be ravenous.

"You'll spoil your appetite," her mom said.

"No, I won't."

"It's fine," her mom said. "Do as you see fit. Just know that when you're sitting at the dinner table, miserably forcing down food that you don't want, you'll have no one to blame but yourself. And don't eat any olives."

"We don't have olives."

Vanessa's mom widened her eyes. *"Exactly."*

Sometimes Vanessa wished that her dad lived closer. Other times she felt like one parent was already more than she could handle. She waited until her mom left the room, then closed the fridge without taking anything.

Sterling came in and said, "Dad says it's your turn now."

Vanessa grabbed the iPad from him and ran up to her bedroom. She didn't make her bed every day, or even

most days, but she'd done it this morning so that when her dad called, he'd see how tidy and responsible she was. "Hi, Daddy!"

She propped the tablet against some pillows and saw her father beam and wave at through the screen. "How's my baby girl?"

Vanessa sort of didn't want to call her father "daddy" anymore. She felt too old for it. She was in middle school now, after all, and she didn't feel like a person who said "daddy." She once had been, but now she wasn't anymore.

But she still said it when she talked to him, because it seemed to make him happy to have a little girl who said "daddy," and she never wanted to make him sad.

"I'm good," Vanessa told him. She wracked her brain for appropriately good news. "I got an A on the science test."

"Attagirl." She could see him roll up the sleeves of his pajamas and take a sip from a mug she'd given him last Father's Day. She could imagine the lavender tea scent that she knew would be wafting out of it.

"And I'm going to the movies this weekend," Vanessa said. "With Rosalie and Honore."

"Who?" her dad asked.

"You know, they're the identical twins. They always do everything together? They once pretended they could

read each other's minds for the talent show, and everyone believed them? Remember them?"

Vanessa thought Rosalie and Honore had a perfect life. They both had a built-in best friend.

"Uh-huh . . ." her dad said.

"You've never met them."

He had never met most of her friends. It wasn't his fault.

"How's my pal Bailey?" he asked cheerily. Bailey was the one friend who he definitely knew.

"Remember how I told you that we're kinda in a fight?" Vanessa said, and he made a noise of agreement. "Well, we're still kinda in a fight."

"That's hard," her dad said.

"I hate it. And I don't get it. Everything was fine and now it's just . . . not. What should I do?"

"Are you asking for my advice as an officer or as a dad?" he asked.

"Either. Both."

Her dad didn't say anything for a long moment, and she thought maybe he didn't know how to respond. Then she realized it was just that the screen had frozen.

"I can't hear you," Vanessa said patiently. "Daddy. Dad. Dad. I can't hear you."

The pixels on the screen scrambled and then settled, and her father seemed to move in fast-forward as the image caught up to real-time. He hadn't noticed that they'd been cut off and was already midsentence.

"—my soldiers get into disagreements with one another, often I'll call them in to my office and have them talk it out. Get them each to express what their issues are with the other—not just snip at each other, but actually say, *you did this thing, and it upset me for this reason.* And then we talk about what they can do to work together better going forward, respect each other more, find compromises. Sometimes I'll give them a task to collaborate on. Teamwork builds trust."

"*That's* how you solve problems in the military? Really?" Vanessa asked.

"Really."

"I thought you'd, like, blow stuff up."

"Force is a last resort," her dad said. "Plus, these are our own people we're talking about. None of them are the enemy. Just like you and Bailey are not enemies."

"I guess," Vanessa said.

Her dad winced. "Stop picking the skin on your cuticles."

"Sorry." Vanessa hadn't even noticed she'd been doing it.

"It makes me sad to see you hurt yourself."

"I already *said* sorry." What more did he want from her? It wasn't like she was picking at her cuticles because she *wanted* to hurt herself, or wanted to make him feel sad.

Vanessa wished she could make whatever time she and her dad had together perfect for him.

"How are *you* doing?" Vanessa asked.

"Oh, you're so sweet to ask. I'm pretty good. Tired! I hit up the gym twice today. I've got my PT test coming up next week so I'm trying to whip myself into shape. You might not be able to see it, but your dad's an old man, Vanessa."

"Oh, don't worry, I can see it," Vanessa replied. Her dad stuck his tongue out at her, and she stuck out her tongue right back.

Her mind drifted a little as he went into way too much detail about how he was training for his upcoming fitness test and how his whole unit was doing extra workouts this week because someone named (or nicknamed?) Mini Mark had failed a practice PT and how the best elliptical machine at the gym was *still* down, can you believe it?

This was a typical answer from her father. He talked a lot, but he didn't share many details about his actual work. But Vanessa wasn't naive, and she knew that war—

or peacekeeping, whatever they wanted to call it—could be dangerous.

Her dad wasn't in a combat role. He was a logistics officer, which meant he kept the base properly stocked with food and fuel and vehicles and uniforms. "I'm the guy who makes sure we have enough ice cream," he always told Vanessa and Sterling.

But he was also the guy who made sure they had enough bullets. And if anyone ever wanted to attack a U.S. military base, they wouldn't distinguish between the people who were and weren't supposed to be in combat roles.

Thinking about her dad being in danger, or putting other people in danger, made Vanessa feel very, very far away from him. Much farther than the actual miles and oceans that stood between them. It wasn't something she'd thought about when she was a little kid and her parents lived together and all her friends were military brats, just like her. But here in Edgewood Falls, a military family was unusual. When she told kids here what her dad did, they would ask if she worried about him. It hadn't even occurred to her that she was supposed to worry until they started asking.

As her dad wound down whatever he was saying about push-ups, Vanessa struggled to think of another

conversational topic. She suspected that this was why Sterling followed baseball. He didn't seem to be genuinely interested in the sport. At least, he never talked about it with anybody else. But he and their father could discuss it for hours. Sterling had a big collection of baseball cards, but all of them had been presents from their father. Vanessa had never seen him buy a baseball card for himself.

Vanessa was always waiting for her next call with her dad, but then when it happened, she never knew quite what to say. Probably she should start following baseball, too. She'd tried before. It was just really, really boring.

She could hear her dad try to hide a yawn. It was six hours later where he was. When Vanessa spent last summer vacation with him, it took her a full week to get used to the time change. She'd kept falling asleep in the middle of the afternoon. "Is it your bedtime?" she asked.

"I'm afraid it is," he said. "Wish you were here with me, sweetheart. I loved having you here. You'll come back next winter break, right? We can go back to that bakery and get you another Schokolade mit Schlagsahne."

"Of course." That was German for *hot chocolate with whipped cream*. It was the first phrase Vanessa had committed to memory when her dad told her he was going to be based in Germany for a few years.

"It can't come soon enough. Take care of yourself. Good luck with Bailey. Keep me posted. I love you."

"I love you, too, Daddy."

Vanessa set down the tablet and thought about her father's advice. *Talk it out.* Actually go up to Bailey and *ask* why she was mad, and then find a way to make it better.

She could do that. In fact, she *would* do it, just as soon as she got to school tomorrow. She'd apologize for whatever it was, and then, finally, this nightmare could end.

CHAPTER 6

Today was the day. The Winning Back Bailey Day. Vanessa dressed in her lucky pair of socks, a T-shirt that she'd painted at Bailey's house, leggings that were a Bailey hand-me-down, and even a Gibby Giraffe headband that she dug up from the bottom of her dresser.

"You look weird," Sterling said over breakfast.

"Sterling," their mother said.

"Sorry," said Sterling. "You look *unique*."

Vanessa didn't care. She wasn't trying to look normal. She was trying to remind Bailey what they meant to each other. Because it seemed like Bailey must have forgotten. Maybe Vanessa did something to upset her, and then her new friends showed up looking all shiny and cute, and somewhere in there, Bailey forgot why her friendship with Vanessa mattered. But she had a whole museum proving to Bailey why their friendship mattered. It was undeniable. Like those two girls in that painting at the museum. They belonged to each other.

"Don't get anywhere near a Great Dane today," their mom said as she dropped off Vanessa and Sterling at the bus stop.

"Okay," they both said. "We won't."

Vanessa's plan had been to talk to Bailey as soon as she got to school, but of course this was the one day that the #5 bus was running late, and by the time she slid into her seat in homeroom, the bell had already rung. Homeroom was the only period that she and Bailey had together in the morning, and there was no time to talk between periods. They were only allowed five minutes to get from one classroom to another, and Edgewood Falls Middle School was enormous. Even if you rushed straight to class, you still might not make it in time, so there was definitely no way to fit in life-or-death conversations about friendship. Vanessa picked the skin around her fingernails and waited.

By lunchtime, Vanessa felt like she was going to burst. She skipped the food line, bulldozed right past her usual table—the table that used to be hers and Bailey's—and

claimed herself a seat at Bailey's new lunch table. She was ready and waiting by the time Bailey got there.

"Hey!" Vanessa said, smiling and waving. "Sit next to me!"

"Okay." Bailey sat down and unwrapped her lunch. "How's it going?"

Vanessa studied her carefully. Bailey was wearing a new pair of earrings, and that was sad—that she'd bought something on a shopping trip that Vanessa wasn't on, that she hadn't sent Vanessa a selfie the first time she'd worn them.

Bailey took a bite of her burrito. It was the same kind of burrito that her dad always made for her: lots of black beans, no cheese, and some vegetables that he always tried to sneak in that she always took out. Bailey's dad had been running a restaurant with his two brothers since they moved here from Mexico more than twenty years ago, so Bailey's lunch was usually a variation of something on the Pancho's menu.

Seeing the burrito gave Vanessa courage. Bailey was still Bailey. Not everything changed.

"Why didn't you invite me to your birthday party?" Vanessa blurted out.

Bailey paused midchew.

Lisa and Kylie swiveled around to look at her.

Vanessa wanted to throw up.

This thing—this not getting invited to a birthday party thing—it had *already happened*. Everybody at the table *knew* it had happened. Maybe everybody in the entirety of Edgewood Falls Middle School knew! Yet somehow Vanessa felt like she was opening up a secret locked box by pointing it out. They all knew it had happened, yet no one was talking about it. Now that she'd gone ahead and put words to it, it was as if she had made it real.

Bailey finished chewing, swallowed, and said, "I had a really small party this year. Dad said I could only invite four people."

"Okay," Vanessa said, but then she shook her head. That explained why *most* people weren't invited, but it still did not explain why she, *Vanessa*, wasn't. Vanessa was special. Wasn't she? Was she crazy or stupid for thinking that she was guaranteed entry to all of Bailey's parties, no matter how small they were?

"Why didn't you *want* to invite me to your party?" Vanessa pressed.

Kylie's mouth was hanging so wide open, Vanessa could have counted her braces.

"I *did* want to," Bailey insisted. "My dad said I couldn't, I told you."

"It's not just the party," Vanessa said. "It's everything. You're different now. You don't care if you sit next to me anymore. You don't like my posts. You don't tell me every time you see Gabe at gymnastics. You don't tell me *anything*."

"I tell you things," Bailey said, like this was all entirely inside Vanessa's head. Like nothing was different, and Vanessa was just making it all up. "What exactly do you want to know?"

"I . . . I don't know! Just stuff! About your life! Whatever you want."

Bailey shook her head. "Oh, please, Ness. Obviously you have some expectation for how much I'm *supposed* to tell you, where I'm *supposed* to sit, how often I'm *supposed* to hang out with you. So why don't you just make a list—or better yet, a whole rule book!—and I'll study it and do exactly what it says. That's what you really want, isn't it?"

Vanessa felt like the world was crumbling around her. She didn't want Bailey to act like a good friend just because she was fulfilling an assignment or something. She wanted Bailey to *want* to be a good friend.

But how could you make somebody want something that they didn't?

"Why do you hate me?" she asked Bailey quietly.

Bailey looked genuinely surprised. "I don't hate you. I don't hate anyone. Except Doc McStubbins." That was the name of the evil alter ego for their favorite YouTube celebrity, Chip Best. Saying that she liked Vanessa more than Doc McStubbins was barely a compliment. It was like saying she preferred Vanessa to dying of a spider bite.

"Fine," Vanessa said. "*Hate* is a strong word." That was something her mother said a lot. "Forget hate. Why are you *mad* at me?"

Bailey's forehead wrinkled. Vanessa knew what that look meant. Either she was confused, or she was trying not to cry, or both.

"I'm sorry," Vanessa said. "For whatever it is. Whatever I did wrong. I'm sorry."

"How can you be sorry if you don't even know what you did?" Bailey asked, rubbing her eyes.

"How can I know what I did if you won't even tell me?" Vanessa countered.

"You weren't here." Bailey's voice was so low Vanessa could hardly hear her.

"What do you mean?" Vanessa asked.

"Last summer!" Bailey said. "You weren't here."

"*That's* why you're mad? Bailey, that wasn't my fault. I had to visit my dad."

"Fine," Bailey said. "You're right. Never mind."

"I mean, he's my *dad*, and he lives thousands of miles away. What was I supposed to do?"

Vanessa felt a surge of anger at her father. If he wasn't stationed so far away, then she wouldn't have had to spend her whole summer on an army base in Germany, and then maybe Bailey would still be her friend.

But then she also felt angry at Bailey, because how could *anyone* blame her for wanting to spend time with her dad on these rare occasions when she could?

"It's not even like we could have done that much if I'd been here," Vanessa pointed out. "You were sick." Bailey had contracted pneumonia last summer, while Vanessa was gone. It sounded miserable, but fortunately she was almost entirely better by the time the school year started.

"Forget it!" Bailey banged her hands down on the table. "It's not about that anyway. It's not one particular thing, okay? It's not because of one thing you did or didn't do. It's just the way you *are*."

"The way I am?" Vanessa repeated. "How am I?"

Lisa spoke up then, even though, to be clear, this had *nothing to do with her.* "You're bossy," she said. "And controlling. And jealous."

Vanessa felt like her heart had stopped.

"Lisa," Bailey said warningly.

"What?" Lisa widened her eyes, the picture of innocence. "She wanted the truth, so I'm telling her the truth. I'm just answering her question."

"You don't have to be mean about it," Bailey said.

"The truth isn't always nice," Lisa said, leaning back in her chair like that wasn't her fault.

Vanessa found her voice. "You don't even know me," she said to Lisa. They hadn't gone to elementary school together. They had only one class together now. If it wasn't for Bailey, Vanessa probably wouldn't even know Lisa's name. How dare Lisa speak about Vanessa as though she was the authority on who or what Vanessa was?

"That's just what Bailey says about you." Lisa shrugged. "Plus, it's gross the way you're always, like, picking at your skin."

Vanessa's face went hot. She stuck her hands under her thighs. "No I'm not."

"Yes, you are," Lisa said. "You were just doing it, like one second ago. We all saw you. Didn't we?"

Kylie and McKenna nodded. Vanessa's chin trembled. She felt like someone had just pantsed her, exposing her ugliest, dumbest, most ill-fitting underpants to the world. Yeah, of course Vanessa knew what her underpants looked like. Of course she knew they were gross and bad. But that didn't mean she was okay with anybody else looking at them and judging them.

She waited for Bailey to say something like *Vanessa doesn't do that. Vanessa is very normal and cute, and everything she does with her hands is normal and cute, too.*

Instead, Bailey opened and closed her mouth like she wasn't sure *what* to say. When she finally spoke, she chose her words carefully. "That's rude," she told Lisa. "When the truth is rude, you don't have to say it."

Which meant that Bailey had noticed Vanessa's picking habit, too. And she thought it was weird, too. And the only reason why she had never said anything was because she wasn't as rude as Lisa.

So it *wasn't* like Vanessa had just been pantsed, after all. It was like she had *never* been wearing pants, and everyone all along had been seeing exactly how ugly her

underwear was—it's just that no one would tell her to her face before today.

Tears stung at Vanessa's eyes. It's one thing if people think you're weird but they're wrong about it. It's another thing entirely if people think you're weird and they're right. They're not making up gossip about you. They're just observing the truth of who you are.

"I don't care about any of that," Bailey said to Vanessa.

Lisa raised her eyebrows and shook her head, like she knew that Bailey *totally* cared about all of that and simply wouldn't admit it.

"I just need you to give me some space, okay? I can't base my entire life around whatever you want." Bailey looked at Vanessa with her eyes open wide, like she was pleading with her. "Ness, we're in *middle school.* I'm *twelve* now. Time passes. Things change."

"I know that," Vanessa shot back. "I've changed. I change all the time."

"Okay, so what exactly have *you* done that's different since we got to middle school?" Bailey asked. "Tell me all about *your* new friends, and *your* new activities and interests. Go on."

The table was silent. All eyes were on Vanessa. She felt hot all over—ashamed, and angry at Bailey for making her

feel ashamed. Was there some *rule* that when you went to middle school, you were supposed to start a whole new life? Whose rule was this, and how come nobody had ever told Vanessa?

"I have a museum now," Vanessa answered finally. Her voice was quiet, uncertain.

"A what?" Lisa asked.

"A museum."

McKenna giggled.

"You can't have a *museum*," Lisa said. "You're just a kid."

"You're just a kid, too," Vanessa shot back.

"I know," Lisa said. "That's why I'm not claiming that I have a museum."

Nothing made any sense. Vanessa was supposed to prove that she was growing up and trying new things—but not in the way that she was actually doing. She was supposed to do it in some *other* way. It felt like whatever Vanessa said or did, she couldn't get it right.

"What kind of museum?" Bailey asked.

She sounded genuinely curious, but Vanessa felt like there was a rock stuck in her throat, and she couldn't answer. She'd tell Bailey, if it was just Bailey. But she didn't want to say anything with the rest of these girls here,

staring at her. They'd make fun of her no matter what the museum was.

"Bailey." Lisa touched her shoulder and sighed. "Don't be so gullible. She doesn't *actually* have a museum. It's like that book where the poor girl pretends she has a hundred dresses and then it turns out they're all just pictures of dresses that she's drawn on scraps of paper."

Vanessa remembered that book. It was called *The Hundred Dresses*. The moral of it was that you shouldn't make fun of people. Clearly this moral had been lost on Lisa.

"I do so have a museum," Vanessa said. "I'm not a liar."

"Okay," said Lisa. "Sure. How many people come to your museum, exactly?"

"Does it have a gift shop?" asked McKenna.

"And a café?" asked Kylie. "Some museums have really good cafés."

"No," Vanessa said in a small voice.

"Well, I think it's great that you're doing something new all by yourself," Bailey said. "I'm proud of you."

Bailey sounded like a parent. It was gross.

"You should come," Vanessa said. "To the museum. I think you'd like it."

"Okay," said Bailey.

"Will you come?" Vanessa asked.

"Maybe someday," Bailey said.

But everyone knew that "maybe someday" meant "never."

Vanessa's plan to win back Bailey had failed. Maybe her dad's advice worked for the military, where there were rules, but it couldn't help with sixth-grade girls.

She'd been wrong. Their relationship *hadn't* been perfect because she, Vanessa, hadn't been perfect. Vanessa had ruined their friendship—the most important thing in the world to her—just by being who she was. And that was that.

Vanessa tossed and turned as she lay in bed that night. Her conversation with Bailey kept running through her head. After lunchtime, all she'd wanted to do was go home and get under the covers and not come out until she was at least twenty-five.

But of course, that wasn't an option. After lunch, she'd had to go to gym and social studies and French. And after that, she had to go to the stupid movies with stupid Rosalie and Honore. And then they wanted to get stupid ice cream. So it was late by the time Vanessa could get home and lie in bed and think about how she'd ruined everything.

She tried not to pick at her skin. She tried really hard. But it kept happening. Especially while they were at the movies, when it was dark and no one was watching her. After lunch, she had vowed to never pick again. But she didn't even make it half an hour. She had a bump on her finger from how she held a pencil, and she picked at it and picked at it so that, by the end of the movie, it was bleeding. It hurt and it was disgusting. The twins' dad gave her a Band-Aid.

It seemed like it should be easy to stop picking. She didn't *want* to do it. It seemed like not wanting it should be enough to stop it.

It was like popcorn at the movies today. During the trailers, Honore kept saying, "I don't want anymore." She kept saying, "I'm gonna make myself sick." She repeated it so many times that it was driving the rest of them up a wall. Vanessa wanted to tell her, "Either eat the popcorn or don't eat the popcorn, just please stop talking about it."

Honore kept eating. Even though she knew she didn't want anymore, even though she knew she was going to make herself sick. Just one piece at a time—but by the end of the movie, she'd finished off the whole carton.

But at least Honore didn't *have* to order popcorn. At least when Honore wasn't at the movies, there was no danger of her eating popcorn until she was sick. Vanessa wasn't so lucky. She couldn't escape her skin.

She needed something else to do with her hands. Origami, maybe.

Vanessa rolled on to her other side and flipped her pillow over and kicked her sheets away.

What had happened at lunch was a nightmare. She'd gone into it hoping that Bailey would tell her what she'd done wrong, and then she could make it right. Well, actually, her first hope had been that Bailey would say something like, "Oh my gosh, I hadn't even noticed that I've been ignoring you. Thanks for pointing that out to me so I can go back to normal!"

But if that couldn't happen, then she'd hoped that Bailey would say something like, "I'm mad at you because of that time when you embarrassed me in front of Gabe." And then Vanessa could apologize for that time when she embarrassed Bailey in front of Gabe, and everything would be okay again.

She'd planned to make the case for their friendship. To prove to Bailey how good it was. To lay out the top ten reasons why Bailey shouldn't leave.

What she hadn't expected was *this*: to be told that she, Vanessa, was bad. She was uncute and weird, and Bailey had stopped being her friend because she didn't deserve Bailey's friendship.

She wondered how long Bailey had known. Had Bailey *always* seen how broken Vanessa was, but for so many years she just put up with it because she was being nice? Did she not notice everything that was wrong with Vanessa until she made other friends and had better people to compare her to? Or had Vanessa herself once been okay, someone you'd want to have in your life, and as time went on she'd just gotten worse and worse until even Bailey couldn't put up with her anymore?

The whole museum was a lie. It told the story of a friendship that Vanessa had believed was true, or wanted to be true. But it wasn't. It was just a story.

Museums were supposed to be for *facts*, weren't they? Like at the Jewish Museum. That *was* a Torah. People *did* wear kippot. They *were* immigrants. Those were truths. Nothing in there was just, like, the museum curator's opinion.

She needed to set the record straight. Now.

Vanessa got out of bed and felt around in her closet for something. She knew it was there, though she hadn't looked at it for a few months. Looking at it made her feel bad. But it belonged in the museum as much as anything else did.

She didn't want to turn on a light. That might attract attention. But she found the item she needed in the very back of her closet, crumpled up into a little ball. She grabbed it and a pair of sneakers and crept downstairs.

From a kitchen drawer, she took out the flashlight that her mom kept in case of a power outage. Vanessa opened the back door to the house quietly, and s-l-o-w-l-y shut it behind her.

She was outside.

She pulled on her sneakers without unlacing them and quickly flicked the flashlight on and off, just to make sure the batteries were still working. They were. She shifted the item onto her arm, took one last look behind her, and took off for the museum at a jog.

The streets were empty and quiet. The lights in all their neighbors' houses were turned off. Even the birds weren't chirping—they must have been asleep, too. Vanessa could hear the quiet buzzing of streetlights and the occasional car motor in the distance. She imagined what people would think if they saw an eleven-year-old girl jogging in her pajamas at midnight. What would the Occam's Razor explanation for her be?

She cut across the park, her feet growing damp from the dewy grass. There was her museum, waiting for her,

steady and silent. Any time of day or night was all the same to a building.

The garbage bag that she'd taped over the window had stayed up, so she ducked underneath it and inside the museum.

It was time to tell the true story of their friendship. Even if it made Vanessa look bad.

She flipped over the label for Item #12: *Shh!: Vol. 1, Issue 1*. And she rewrote it.

I heard Keiko Cho bragging about how she faked a peanut allergy so she could be in Mr. Van Stampfel's class, and I knew this was a perfect story for a gossip magazine. But Bailey didn't want to include it. She said we didn't know for sure whether or not Keiko actually had an allergy and anyway it was none of our business. I told her she could never be a real journalist if she wasn't willing to take risks. I included the story, and then Keiko's mom complained to the principal and he shut it down. Bailey got mad at me because, by insisting that we publish this story, I got us BOTH in trouble.

Good. That was better. That was true.

ITEM #5: FRAGMENT OF A FRIENDSHIP BRACELET

Materials: embroidery thread.
Bailey stitched this bracelet for me over spring break of fourth grade. I had to visit my dad in Virginia, so we didn't see each other for the whole week. I wore it every day for almost a year after that until the knot unraveled. But I didn't make anything for her the whole time I was gone. I didn't even text her.

Vanessa felt guilty as she wrote down all the ways she'd been a bad friend to Bailey, and that felt right. The guilt felt crummy but was exactly what she deserved.

ITEM #23: PLAYBILL FOR ST. EVANGELINE'S ANNUAL CHRISTMAS PAGEANT

Materials: paper.

Bailey played an angel in her church's Christmas pageant, and she was really excited but also super-nervous because she gets stage fright. She was perfect, though. At least she was in the second half of the pageant. I missed the first half because Chip Best was doing a YouTube Live at the same time and I didn't want to leave until he'd answered my question.

And now it was time to add in the new item. The one that hadn't fit before.

Vanessa took the dress, Bailey's dress, and shook it out. It was wrinkled from being stuffed in the back of her closet for so long. She hung it in a large, empty wooden picture frame and wrote a label.

ITEM #28: BAILEY'S CONFIRMATION DRESS

Materials: cotton and polyester.

Bailey loved this dress. I did, too. She wore it to her confirmation, but that was the only time. I asked if I could have it after, but she said no. I asked why, and

she said she might want to wear it again someday. I told her she'd never be able to wear it again because she'd gotten too big. "I'm small enough to wear it," I told her. "You're not. You wouldn't even be able to zip it up."

So she did give it to me. And it fit perfectly. But I never wore it. Because every time I looked at it, I felt bad.

I was mean to Bailey so she would give me what I wanted. And it worked.

Vanessa's stomach roiled as she taped the label next to the hanging dress. She had never talked about that interaction. Nobody who had been there that day ever talked about it. It was like everyone wanted to pretend that it hadn't happened, that Vanessa hadn't purposefully hurt her favorite person in the world.

But you couldn't erase something like that by ignoring it. It just stayed there, rotting everything from the inside.

Vanessa loved Bailey so much, and also sometimes she was terrible to her. How could both those things be true at the same time?

She couldn't blame Bailey for not wanting to be friends anymore.

Vanessa swung her flashlight over the next display case. What other false labels were in there? What else did she need to rewrite, to finally tell the truth?

Then she caught something in the beam of light and stopped. Stepped closer.

There was an item in the display case that she'd never seen before.

She shone the flashlight directly on it, to make sure she wasn't just imagining things in the dark. But it was really there. A chewed-up tennis ball, in the display case behind glass, right in the middle of her Bailey collection. And next to it was a label.

TENNIS BALL

Materials: tennis ball.

Dogs like to chase tennis balls.

"What?" Vanessa whispered.

The placard was messily handwritten on a lined sheet of paper with a ragged edge, torn out of a notebook. It did not look anything like Vanessa's labels. She studied the handwriting, but it didn't look familiar. She had no idea who had put this tennis ball in her display, or why, or what the label meant. None of it made any sense.

But she did know one thing for sure:

Somebody else had found her museum.

CHAPTER 8

Vanessa didn't finish rewriting her labels. She was too spooked by that tennis ball. *Dogs like to chase tennis balls.* Well, sure, that seemed true, but why would someone write that down? Why would they put it inside one of her display cases?

She became suddenly, uncomfortably aware of the fact that it was very dark and she was very alone. Nobody knew where she was. If the tennis ball person—whoever they were—was here in the museum right this second, and if Vanessa was never heard from again, nobody would even know where to start looking for her.

She swung her flashlight around the room, but the beam was too focused and dim and the museum was too big. Someone could be hiding here. In one of the side rooms, under a display, behind the admissions desk. She wouldn't know until it was too late.

She grabbed one of the index cards that she used to label artifacts, and then—in her neat handwriting, not like the scrawl on the tennis ball placard—which, the more that she thought about it, the more likely that seemed to be the handwriting of a crazed criminal—she wrote on it the following sentence:

WHO ARE YOU, AND WHAT ARE YOU DOING IN MY MUSEUM?

And then she ran all the way home.

"Wow, look who finally decided to get out of bed," said Sterling when Vanessa padded into the kitchen the next day.

Vanessa poured herself a glass of orange juice and blinked at the clock on the microwave. 11:23. That *was* late. She'd even missed her chance to wish on 11:11. Vanessa and Bailey always made wishes when the clock said 11:11. Also when the clock said 22:22 (which was military time

for 10:22 at night). Those were the only times of day when all four numerals were the same, and that made them lucky.

Vanessa wondered if Bailey had stopped making 11:11 wishes now that they weren't friends anymore. If she *did* still make them, that would mean she still cared a little bit, right? It would mean she hadn't just forgotten or blocked out everything about their friendship. It would mean that Vanessa was still part of her, every day, if only for one minute.

"I've been up for a while," Vanessa lied, sitting down next to her brother at the kitchen counter. "I was reading in bed." She glanced at her mother, who was making challah French toast, as was their weekend tradition. She wondered if her mother knew that she'd snuck out last night. Sometimes her mom just knew when Vanessa had broken a rule, no matter how carefully Vanessa covered her tracks.

But all her mom said was, "I admire your air of superiority, Sterling. Exactly how much longer than your sister have *you* been awake for?"

"A long time," said Sterling.

"Fifteen minutes," said their mom. "At most."

"I was up for a while before that," said Sterling. "I was reading in bed."

Vanessa kicked him.

"Well, unfortunately you both woke up too late for us to go to services," their mom said.

"We don't go to services," Sterling replied.

Their mom nodded. "Good point. Can't argue with that."

They'd had to go to Shabbat services at Temple Beth Elohim ten Saturdays in the year before Sterling's bar mitzvah. That was the rule at their synagogue—you couldn't have a bar mitzvah if you didn't go to services at least ten times. After services, there were always cookies out in the community hall, and sometimes there was even a whole spread with bagels and lox and different types of cream cheese, but except on days when the food was *really* fancy, it didn't make up for the fact that Saturday morning services were almost three hours long and you couldn't look at your phone the whole time. So after Sterling's bar mitzvah, two years ago, they stopped going.

"We're going to have to start making Shabbat a habit again pretty soon," their mom said. "Vanessa's bat mitzvah is only fourteen months away."

Fourteen months felt like so far in the future that it had nothing to do with anything. But, on the other hand, fourteen months didn't feel like nearly enough time to learn all the Hebrew that Vanessa would be expected to know.

"I already went to services ten times before Sterling's bar mitzvah," Vanessa pointed out. "Can't I just count those as my ten?"

"Nope," said their mom. "They weren't in the year immediately before your bat mitzvah."

Vanessa heaved a deep sigh.

"But *I* don't have to go to ten services in the next year," Sterling said. "Right?"

"No fair," Vanessa objected. "I had to go to his ten. He should have to go to mine."

"That's only because you were too little to stay home alone then," Sterling reminded her. "I'm not."

"What are you going to do home alone while your sister and I are at services?" their mom asked Sterling. "Sleep until noon?"

Sterling shrugged. "Yeah, maybe."

Their mom rolled her eyes dramatically and ruffled his hair. "Might as well get used to the fact that I'm raising two teenagers," she said.

"*I'm* not a teenager," said Vanessa.

"Not yet," said her mom, "but you will be."

Vanessa frowned. "So what?"

"Teenagers need a lot of sleep. It has to do with how your body is developing. When I was in high school, sometimes I would sleep well into the afternoon!"

Vanessa truly, deeply hated it when her mom said the word "body." Also "developing."

Her mom plated the first batch of French toast and put it in front of them. "Get it while it's hot," she said, just as she did every Saturday.

"Is it, like, a *rule*?" Vanessa asked, shaking powdered sugar over her French toast.

"Is what a rule?" asked Sterling.

"Like, do teenagers *have* to sleep really late? All of them? Are all teenagers exactly the same, and when someone becomes a teenager you know exactly what they're going to do just because of how old they are?"

"No," her mother said, starting a second batch of French toast. "There are no rules about how anyone has to be a teenager. There are no rules about how to be a person at all."

"I sleep later now that I'm fourteen than I did when I was your age," Sterling observed.

Somehow this annoyed Vanessa, even though she had literally no reason to care about when her brother slept. It

was like he was playing right into their expectations, and he didn't even mind.

"Would you two have any interest in going for a bike ride today?" their mom asked, sitting down with them. "The weather's finally nice enough."

What Vanessa really wanted was to go back to her museum, to see if the tennis ball writer had responded to her note. But there probably hadn't been enough time for that yet.

"Can we ride to the art store?" Vanessa asked. "I want to get origami paper."

"Sure," Mom agreed. "We can take Woodrow across to Northcross so we can avoid the hill—"

"Not the art store in the Pancho's shopping center," Vanessa interrupted. "Please. Can we go to Papercuts instead?"

"It's a longer ride," her mom reminded her.

"I don't mind." Vanessa would bike any distance if it meant not having to go past Bailey's family's restaurant.

So after the three of them finished eating, they found their bike helmets, pumped air into their tires, and headed out on the road.

Vanessa couldn't bike anymore without thinking about her picking problem, because a bike ride was actually how

it had begun. On a ride almost two years ago, she'd fallen off her bike, skinning her knee and elbow. It bled a lot, but she had been very brave and barely even cried. Her mom cleaned it up and bandaged the wounds.

But a couple days later, as her skin began to regrow, Vanessa started to tear at it with her fingernails. She was just trying to even it out, trying to get rid of the flakes of skin that were itchy and stuck out. But pulling off the flakes felt so good, for some reason that she couldn't describe, so she kept casting about for more and more skin to pull off.

The wounds on her elbow and knee took ages to heal. Every time they scabbed over, she picked at the edges of the scab until it came all the way off, leaving raw, bloody, tender skin behind.

Eventually there was nothing left to peel off, but there were still faint scars from where she'd fallen. She could see them even now. And it was after that that her fingers starting seeking out other things to pick at. Like perfectly healthy skin around her fingernails, which she dug into again and again until it wasn't so healthy anymore.

On this bike ride with her mom and Sterling, as with every bike ride in the past two years, Vanessa had the fleeting thought that she could fall off on purpose. She didn't *want* to. She hated being in pain as much as anyone else

did. And the sight of blood grossed her out. So she wasn't going to do it. But she yearned for a really good scab to pick at. And she hated that about herself. Lisa was right about her.

She was going to stop picking. She *was*. She was going to get a bunch of origami paper, and she was going to fold cranes instead. And then she would have beautiful skin and everyone would like her.

They biked past a mailbox, which inspired their mom to tell them a story about some guy who'd stuck a love letter in the mail, chickened out, tried to break open the mailbox to steal his letter back, and wound up with a paper cut that got infected and he had to go to the hospital—where it turned out that the woman he'd written the love letter to was his emergency room doctor!

"Don't mail a love letter unless you're a hundred percent sure you won't want it back," their mother concluded.

"Okay," said Vanessa and Sterling. "We won't."

Their mom worked for a local news station. She wasn't an "on-air personality"—her face wasn't on billboards or the sides of buses—instead, she did research in the news room so the on-air personalities would have stories to report on. Vanessa's mom's area of expertise was what she called "human interest." She found true stories about

unusual things happening to people all over the world, and she wrote them up so the on-air personalities could present them in sixty seconds or less, usually immediately before a commercial break and followed by a one-sentence moral.

They got to Papercuts and Vanessa found an origami pack with 144 squares of paper, each one of them beautiful. Even if this didn't stop her from picking at her skin, she was still excited to make things with the paper.

Their ride home *was* long, but Vanessa couldn't complain because she was the one who wanted to go all the way to Papercuts. Their route took them past the park, on the other side of which was the cul-de-sac, at the far end of which was her museum.

Vanessa's eyes were drawn toward it. It was still mostly blocked by trees, still on a little dead-end street that almost nobody would bother going down, but now that she knew it was there, she couldn't imagine how anyone could miss it.

She fought the urge to jump off her bike and run into the museum, find out if the tennis ball was still there, see if the tennis ball person had replied to her note. Of course she couldn't do that, not with her mom and brother right there.

But she couldn't help but stare at the museum from

across the park, and her mom noticed. "It's an eyesore," she said.

"What?" Vanessa faced front again as they cycled past it.

"That old building," her mother clarified. "The city should really do something about it. They were supposed to tear it down ages ago. It's too bad they let it fall into such disrepair. It must have been something really special when it was built. Somebody obviously put a lot of time and thought into it, once upon a time."

"Yeah," said Vanessa. "Once upon a time."

Her mother shrugged and shifted gears. "But I guess all things must come to an end, right?"

And it seemed like that was true. Vanessa just didn't know why.

After they finished riding their bikes, Sterling took a shower and their mom cleaned up from breakfast and Vanessa ran over to her museum because riding past it without going inside wasn't good enough.

She went straight to the tennis ball. It was still on display, as if it belonged here, in the middle of this exhibit

about Bailey. But the note that Vanessa had scribbled last night had been replaced with a new note, written in the same messy handwriting as the words *Dogs like to chase tennis balls.*

This new note said: *Meet me here at 3 P.M. tomorrow.*

And Vanessa knew that might be a bad idea, maybe even as bad as mailing a love letter that you didn't really want to send. But she also knew that she was going to do it anyway.

CHAPTER 9

Vanessa squirmed all through Hebrew school and all through brunch afterward. She was just about to head to the museum for her three o'clock meeting when her dad called. He had the worst timing. This was not one of their scheduled calls, which meant he had something specific he wanted to discuss with her.

What he wanted to discuss was Bailey. "Did you two have that talk on Friday?" he asked.

"Uh-huh." Vanessa didn't want to rehash that horrible cafeteria scene. What she *wanted* was to go to her museum. She paced around her room holding her phone, hoping he would get the hint that *she was busy*.

"And did you patch things up?" her dad pressed.

Vanessa thought about Bailey saying, *I don't hate you . . . I just need you to give me some space.* But that wasn't what *Vanessa* needed. Why did Bailey's needs matter more than Vanessa's?

What Vanessa wanted from Bailey was simple and impossible. She wanted to be Bailey's favorite person. She wanted Bailey to tell her everything and include her in everything and invite her to everything, no matter how many times she couldn't come. She wanted Bailey to do all these things because *she* wanted to, never because she was taking pity on Vanessa or repaying a favor. Vanessa wanted to be exactly who she was, un-cute parts and all, and have Bailey think she was perfect. She wanted Bailey to be like a video game character, who just swayed in place until the next time Vanessa logged on to play again.

Maybe these weren't fair things to want. But she wanted them anyway, so badly that it tore her up inside.

"She's mad at me because I went to visit you last summer," Vanessa answered her dad, knowing this wasn't one hundred percent true, but either it would make him feel guilty for living so far away or it would make him think poorly of Bailey, and either of those options seemed satisfying.

But all he said was, "Maybe she missed you."

"But I'm here now," Vanessa pointed out. "If she missed so much, then shouldn't she be glad that I'm back?"

"Maybe she changed while you were gone," her dad suggested. "Maybe you changed, too. It's okay. That happens. Sometimes we change and then we don't have the same sort of relationship with someone that we used to. It's nobody's fault."

But that had nothing to do with Bailey. Vanessa knew that he was really talking about himself and her mom.

For Vanessa's whole life, her dad basically had to go wherever the army sent him. When she was little, the whole family would follow her father wherever he was stationed. They'd spent time in Virginia Beach and Fort Hood and even one year out in Hawaii. She and Sterling would play with the other kids who lived on base and join their mom on shopping trips to the commissary. They made friends fast and lost them just as quickly, as either they would move or the other kids would.

When Vanessa was four, her dad was deployed to Afghanistan for a year. Apparently this was a terrible time for the rest of them: Sterling started wetting the bed again, even though he'd outgrown that ages ago, and he acted out in school. Vanessa didn't remember any of that; she just remembered that her dad didn't come home for

her preschool dance recital, even though at the time she thought it was the most important thing in the world.

Then her dad came home, and things were supposed to be better but somehow they just got worse. He and her mom fought constantly. He deployed again eighteen months later, and this time their mom packed up the kids and moved them all to Ohio, where she'd grown up. She got the job at the news station, and her parents took care of Vanessa and Sterling after school. Nobody wet the bed, and their mom bought a very big and very heavy couch that took three professionals to move.

When her dad came back to America after that deployment, he didn't move into their house in Ohio. He couldn't, because they didn't live close enough to a military base. He visited, traveling back and forth from Fort Knox whenever he could, but he never lived with them again.

He tried to convince Vanessa's mom that the family should join him at whatever base the military sent him to next. Vanessa's mom pointed out that her couch would be very hard to move.

Vanessa's dad left. Vanessa, Sterling, and her mom stayed put. The couch did, too.

They weren't technically divorced. Technically, they were separated. Vanessa didn't fully understand what

the difference was. Whatever you called it, they weren't really married.

If her parents hadn't split up, then Vanessa's whole family would probably be living in Germany right now. She wouldn't be in a fight with Bailey. But she also wouldn't have ever gotten close enough to Bailey to be in this sort of a fight with her. Bailey would have been her friend the year that her dad was deployed and they stayed in Ohio, and maybe they'd still text each other today, but probably not.

Would that be a better life?

When they'd visited their dad last summer, Vanessa and Sterling had toured many sites of Germany: castles and historical places and museums. But none of them was Vanessa's museum.

"What are you doing there?" her dad asked her, squinting at the screen. "Is that origami?"

"Yeah," Vanessa said. "I taught myself to make a butterfly yesterday. See?" She held it up.

He nodded. "Looking good, honey. Such an artist!"

She checked the time. It was almost three already. "Daddy," she said, "I have to go. I have, like, a project that I need to work on."

"Sure thing, baby," he said. "I'll see you in just a few weeks. I'm counting down the days!"

After they hung up, she ran up to Sterling's room to ask: "Remind me why Dad is coming home?"

"For Passover," Sterling replied without looking up from his book.

"But *he's* not Jewish," Vanessa pointed out. "Why's he flying back from Germany for a holiday that's not even his?"

Sterling shrugged. "Because we're a family?" This was something their parents both said sometimes, like it explained away everything. "And anyway, he's deploying again right after."

"Boo," Vanessa said. She'd known that her dad's next deployment was looming on the horizon, but she had purposefully forgotten how close it was. When her dad deployed, he couldn't just stay on his base in Germany, which was as safe as being in the armed forces could be. Instead, he had to go to active war zones and work there for months, sometimes even a full year.

"Dad always comes to see us right before he deploys," Sterling reminded her.

"Yeah, I know." Vanessa just wished her dad could come visit for fun, without it being the harbinger of danger.

The clock on Sterling's bureau read 2:58. She didn't have time to think about this. "I gotta go." She ran downstairs, out the door, and all the way to the museum. She was huffing and puffing by the time she pushed her way through the garbage bag curtain. And there, on the other side, right in the middle of her museum, was the person who had found it.

"You're late," said Eli Schaefer.

CHAPTER 10

Vanessa had never seen Eli outside of Temple Beth Elohim. "What are you doing here?" she demanded.

"We had a meeting at three," he replied.

"I know," she said, "I just didn't know the meeting was with *you*."

"I didn't know the meeting would be with you, either," said the class clown. "I like what you've done with the place. Really spruced it up."

"Who told you it was okay to come inside my museum?" asked Vanessa, putting her hands on her hips.

"It's not *your* museum," he said. "I've known about this place for ages. If anything, *you've* been coming inside *my* museum."

"I don't believe you," said Vanessa. "If you'd known about this place for ages, then how come it looked like such a mess when I showed up? There was trash everywhere!"

"Just because I knew about it doesn't mean I was going to clean it up," said Eli. "Anyway, I hadn't come over here in a few months. I used to walk my dog here."

"That's why you left the tennis ball?" Vanessa pointed to it, in its display case. *Dogs like to chase tennis balls.*

"Yup. That was one of Einstein's."

"You named your dog Einstein?"

"Yeah. He was the dumbest dog you've ever met. It was ironic."

Vanessa didn't totally know what that meant, but she wasn't going to give Eli the satisfaction of asking.

"But you haven't walked your dog in a few months?" Vanessa asked.

"Why would I? It'd be weird to walk a ghost." Eli bit his thumbnail.

"Oh," Vanessa said. She blinked. "I'm sorry."

"Hey," Eli said, "what do you call a funeral ship?"

Vanessa shook her head.

"A sea hearse!" he crowed

"Okay," said Vanessa.

"Get it? It's like 'sea horse,' only a hearse is the car that coffins go in?"

"Yeah," Vanessa said, "I got it. Did you put Einstein on a funeral ship?"

"No. We buried him in the backyard." Eli rubbed the bridge of his nose.

It was surprising to Vanessa that she'd gone to Hebrew school with Eli since second grade, yet she'd never known that he had a dog until he didn't have one anymore. He'd always just been "the funny one." Not "the funny one with a dog."

"What's the deal with that painting?" Eli asked, gesturing at the park scene, with its marble statue and the two girls and their picnic.

"I found it in that side room."

"It's cool," Eli said, and Vanessa felt a twinge of satisfaction: Maybe he'd found this place before she did, but he hadn't explored it, really. He hadn't made it his own. "What's it doing here?"

Vanessa shrugged. "I'm guessing it used to belong to the museum, back when this place was open." They both looked at it. The artist had signed her name in the lower right-hand corner: *Maria*.

"So . . ." Eli said, fiddling with the stack of index cards that Vanessa had left at the front desk. "You've probably guessed why I asked you to meet me here." When Vanessa didn't say anything, he went on: "I want to do a museum exhibition about Einstein."

"Oh! Here?" Vanessa looked at the chewed-up tennis ball, the sloppy handwriting and the uninteresting information that it provided. A whole exhibition of stuff like *that*? "I'm sorry, but this is the Museum of Bailey. My ex–best friend," she added.

Eli wrinkled his nose at her. "It's a big museum."

"Well, Bailey and I had a big friendship." Vanessa wasn't even totally sure why she felt so strongly about not sharing, except that she and Eli didn't have anything in common. How could he possibly understand what she was trying to do with this museum? He'd just fill it up with his usual jokey stuff. "A dog isn't the same thing as a person," she explained as gently as possible.

"Yeah," Eli said, "and *dead* isn't the same thing as *in a fight*."

"You can get another dog," Vanessa pointed out.

"And you can get another friend."

"I *have* other friends!"

"Then why are you here alone?"

Vanessa crossed her arms. Because she didn't trust anyone else as much as Bailey, was why. Because there were special things that you shared only with certain people, but you didn't just go around sharing everything with everyone.

Eli picked up the gross tennis ball from its display case and tossed it from hand to hand. "All I'm saying is—is Bailey really worth all of this?"

"Of course she is."

"She doesn't seem like she's worth it."

Eli was so annoying. No way was Vanessa going to share her museum with someone who didn't even see how important Bailey was. "Haven't you *looked* at the exhibit?" She marched around, grabbing up artifacts and thrusting them at Eli. "Look, here are our floor plans for the tree house we wanted to build. Here's a mix-tape she made me. An actual *tape*! Do you have any idea how hard it was for her to even *find* a tape recorder? Here's the pop-up card that she made me for Valentine's Day last year. See, you open it, and a heart actually *pops out at you*!" She shook the construction paper in his face.

"Hey," said Eli, "what's the best color for a heart?" He didn't wait for Vanessa to answer before crowing: "Beat red!"

Vanessa glared at him.

"Get it? 'Beet red' is a color, but 'beat red' is what hearts do?"

"*You're* the one who's not getting it," Vanessa said. "Bailey made all these amazing things for me or with me. How could you even think that she's not worth it?"

"Look, I don't know her—"

"Clearly," Vanessa interrupted.

"—But if she's just going to walk away from you after all those years of friendship, after tree houses and mixtapes and all of that, then how great could she possibly be?"

"Bailey had good reasons for leaving," Vanessa said, defending her. "It was my fault."

"What did you do?" Eli asked. "Betray her? Backstab her? Blackmail her? Didn't know you had it in you, Lepp."

Vanessa looked at the labels that she'd rewritten last night. She looked at Bailey's dress. "None of your business."

"Actually, when you create an entire museum exhibition about it, you make it my business."

"The museum exhibition is for me," Vanessa said. "You weren't supposed to see it. Nobody's supposed to see it. It's private. You're trespassing."

"In that case, we're *both* trespassing," Eli said. "And it's a museum, not a diary. Museums are meant to be visited and seen and shared."

"Says who?"

"Says everyone! That's, like, the definition of a museum! That's why I want to put my Einstein stuff in here. He was a really good dog. So I want to share him with other people. I shouldn't be the only one who knows about what a good dog he was."

Vanessa heard Eli's voice catch, and she looked at him. Really looked. And what she saw was not the kid in her Hebrew school class, or the stranger who had infiltrated her secret museum.

What she saw was a person who had lost someone he loved. Just like her.

Maybe she and the class clown *did* have something in common, after all.

"Okay," said Vanessa.

"Okay?" Eli repeated.

"Okay, you can put up an Einstein exhibit. Meet back here after Hebrew school on Tuesday, bring more of his

stuff with you, and we'll set it up. It can be the Museum of Bailey and of Eli's Slobbery Dog."

"Hey, how do you know he was slobbery?" Eli asked, but he was smiling.

"Because I saw that tennis ball! Now come on, let me show you how to curate a museum exhibit."

CHAPTER 11

At Hebrew school on Tuesday afternoon, Vanessa and Eli kept exchanging meaningful looks across the classroom. It was nice, having a secret project with somebody else. Vanessa hadn't had one of those in a long time.

After Hebrew school, Vanessa's carpool dropped her off at home. Her mom wasn't back from work yet, and Sterling was out somewhere, or just silently holed up in his room. He'd been doing that a lot recently. Vanessa grabbed a roll of tape, a box of markers, and the biggest sheets of blank paper she could find and headed out to the museum. Eli was supposed to meet her there with a bunch of Einstein artifacts, and now that there were going to be multiple sections to the museum, Vanessa wanted to make signs establishing where the different exhibitions started and ended.

She ducked through the trash bag curtain and found that Eli hadn't arrived yet.

But somebody else had.

"Sterling?" Vanessa yelled. "What are *you* doing here?"

She dropped her art supplies in a heap and marched over to the display case that her brother was leaning against. He grinned at her, trying to play it cool, but his cheeks had gone pink. Clearly he knew that showing up here was not actually cool, not at all.

"I overheard you and Eli plan to meet here," Sterling said, "so I thought I'd come, too."

"You *overheard*?" Vanessa repeated. "You mean you eavesdropped. You followed me here on Sunday and then you eavesdropped on my private conversation?"

Sterling shrugged, which meant *yes*. "It's a free country," he said, which was the worst excuse ever. Their mom didn't even allow them to use that phrase in the house—she said it was such an oversimplification.

"I'll tell Mom," threatened Vanessa.

"That I said 'it's a free country'?" asked Sterling.

"That you followed me and spied on me."

"Okay," Sterling said, "then I'll tell Mom that you've been breaking and entering an abandoned building."

"I haven't been breaking anything," Vanessa protested. "That window was already busted when I got here."

"But you *have* been entering," said Sterling.

"So what?" Vanessa said. "It's—" She bit her lip.

Sterling laughed. "Were you going to say 'It's a free country'?"

Vanessa glared at him.

"This whole place is going to get demolished soon anyway," Sterling reminded her. "There's a sign outside."

But that sign was old. They'd forgotten to tear this place down for years. Maybe they would keep forgetting forever.

"This is *my* thing," Vanessa said. "Why don't you go do your own thing? With your own friends?"

Sterling blushed and opened his mouth, but before he had the chance to reply, a voice came from the window. "Wait 'til you see what I've got," Eli was saying as he pushed past the trash bag entryway. "I printed a bunch of photos of Einstein when he was a puppy, and I got his leash and his water bowl and his favorite pillow and—oh, hey, man! What's up? I'm Eli."

"He already knows who you are," Vanessa said. "Because he was spying on us."

"I'm Sterling," said Sterling.

"My brother," added Vanessa.

"Okay, yeah, I thought you looked familiar. I must've seen you around temple before." Eli dumped his dog stuff next to the display case that Vanessa had cleared out for his use. "What are you going to curate an exhibition about, Sterling?"

"My baseball card collection," Sterling said, at the same time that Vanessa said, "Nothing."

Eli came over to peer at Sterling's display, and for the first time, Vanessa looked at it, too. And it was actually . . . not bad. Maybe even kind of good.

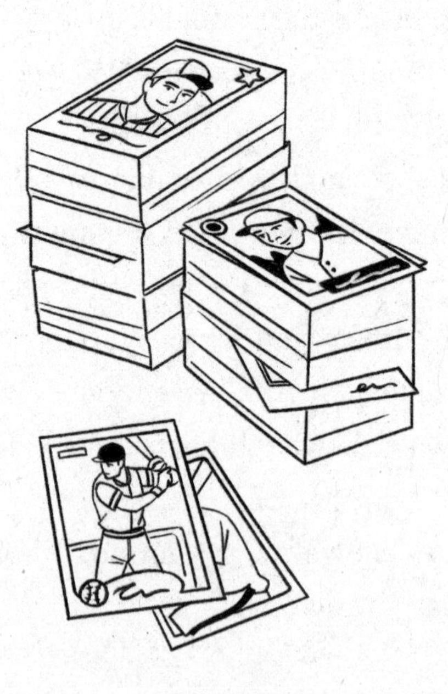

"So, there are tons of different ways to organize baseball cards, obviously," Sterling said. "What I've done so far is divided them up by team, and I've organized the teams geographically. See, the far left side of the display case has the Dodgers and the Giants, and then over on the other side are the Yankees and the Red Sox. And right now I'm organizing the cards chronologically within each team. Steve Carlton is the oldest player I have. His card's actually pretty valuable. But, I don't know, I'm thinking maybe instead I should pull out all the rookie cards and do a separate display just of those."

"The nice thing about a museum is that you can move stuff around," Vanessa said. "So you can do a special exhibit just on rookie cards, and then later you could do a special exhibit just on the Chicago Cubs or whatever. I've already reorganized my Bailey exhibition a few times."

"So I *can* have a display case here?" Sterling asked.

"I didn't say that."

"Sure he can," said Eli. "Why not?" He and Sterling high-fived.

"Eli, you're not in charge of the museum," Vanessa pointed out.

"I've been coming here a lot longer than you have," Eli pointed out.

"Yeah, but it never even occurred to you to actually use the museum as a museum until I showed up, so I think it's fair that I get to decide what happens here."

"Bossy," whispered Sterling.

"Sexist," Vanessa shot back.

"Wait, what?" said Eli. "'Bossy' is sexist?"

Sterling nodded. "Our mom says that when guys are authoritative, they get called 'leaders,' but when girls are authoritative, they get called 'bossy,' and treating guys and girls differently for the same behavior is sexism."

"Oh, okay." Eli shrugged. "Well, then I don't know the word for it, but, Vanessa, it does seem like sometimes you don't like things just because they weren't your idea, and that doesn't seem like a good enough reason not to do something. Your brother's cards seem cool. Hey, Sterling, why did the baseball player spend only a couple minutes at the supermarket?"

"Uh, I don't know?" Sterling said.

"Because," Eli crowed, "it was a *short stop*!" The two of them high-fived again.

Vanessa looked at the boys. They were being a lot nicer than Lisa had been at lunch on Friday . . . but what they were saying was not all that different. Lisa had called her bossy, too. And Bailey had accused Vanessa of always

telling her what she was and wasn't supposed to do. And she'd also said that was the reason why they weren't friends any more. *It's just the way you are*, she'd said.

Vanessa wanted to become the sort of person who new Bailey, middle school Bailey, wanted to be friends with. She would change who she was. She would turn over a whole new leaf.

So she said too Sterling, "Okay."

"Okay?"

"Okay, you can curate an exhibit."

She was still worried that her brother might not do it right. But he broke into a big grin, and that made her smile, too.

"Hey," Eli said, "if we're going to have a bunch of different exhibitions, we should display Maria's painting, too."

"Definitely," Vanessa agreed.

Together, they moved the artwork over to the back wall, where it could best be seen. Sterling let out a long whistle of admiration.

"I wonder how old it is," Eli said.

"It can't be *that* old," Sterling said. "Look at how the people in it are dressed. It couldn't be older than the 1960s, maybe."

"That's still pretty old," Vanessa said.

"Not compared to, like, Michelangelo or da Vinci."

Sterling stared at it some more. "I wonder where that place is. If it even exists."

"I wonder who Maria was," Vanessa said. "Or is? if this painting really is from the 1960s, then maybe she's still alive." She tried to look it up, but she wasn't getting good service, so the results took too long to load. She put her phone away. "I'll figure it out later. Right now, we've got work to do."

And so until the sun set, the three of them worked on their exhibits. Sterling played music off his phone for them all to listen to while he arranged his baseball cards. Eli sat cross-legged on the floor, his tongue poking a tiny bit out of his mouth as he painstakingly wrote up legends for the Einstein items that he'd carried over today. Vanessa worked on the big signs, four of them now:

BAILEY

EINSTEIN

BASEBALL CARDS

MARIA

Occasionally the three of them called out to one another for help—"Do you spell 'canine' with a 'c' or a 'k'?" asked Eli; and, "Is Milwaukee east or west of Atlanta?" asked Sterling—but mostly they just quietly did their own things. The museum felt more full than it ever had before. Vanessa was surprised to find that she liked it.

"I googled Maria," Vanessa told Eli and Sterling. They were creating a big map of the museum on a white-board that Eli had brought in. They drew the floor plan with a permanent marker, and then the names and locations of the various exhibits with dry-erase markers, so they could change them around as they needed to.

"The artist?" Eli asked. "Did you find out anything?"

Vanessa shook her head. "I searched for 'Maria + painting' and 'Maria + two girls picnic fountain statue' and 'Maria + Edgewood Falls.' Nothing came up. Or, like, a zillion things came up, but none of them were useful. Turns out there are a lot of Marias who have painted things. And there are a lot of Marias in Edgewood Falls. There are even a lot of Marias who have painted things *and* live in Edgewood Falls."

"Well, yeah," Sterling said. "What did you expect? Plus, we don't know if Maria lived in Edgewood Falls, or if she ever even visited here. For all we know, she lives in Tokyo or Qatar or Siberia, and her painting got shipped here and she's never heard of our town in her life."

Vanessa sighed. Her brother was right, which she really hated. Still, that didn't stop her from wanting an explanation for the painting, why it was here in her museum, or what happened next for the two friends within it.

"Maybe Maria's in jail," Eli suggested.

"Why would she be in jail?" Vanessa asked.

Eli waggled his eyebrows. "Because she had *a brush* with the law? Get it? Like a paintbrush?"

Vanessa didn't even bother to roll her eyes, but her brother responded with a full guffaw and a fist bump. She wished Bailey was here.

"There are too many boys in this museum," Vanessa announced. "I'm the only girl, and the only person who doesn't have a *seriously* bad sense of humor. I feel outnumbered."

"Well, then I also feel outnumbered," said Sterling. "I'm the only high schooler."

"Then why don't you go hang out with other high schoolers?" Vanessa shot back.

Sterling shrugged and mumbled something that Vanessa couldn't make out.

"I'm outnumbered, too," Eli piped up. "I'm the only person who's not a member of your family."

"What I'm saying," Vanessa explained, "is that I want to invite a friend to curate the museum with us."

"*Please* don't tell me you mean Bailey," Sterling said, setting down the blue dry-erase marker.

Vanessa had totally meant Bailey.

"Bailey's the worst," Eli agreed.

"You've never even met her!" Vanessa snapped.

"She stopped being friends with you for no good reason." Eli shrugged. "That's all I need to know. She's the worst."

"That's not true. Did you even look at my exhibition? I explain it all in there. She had plenty of reasons." *I'm bossy and controlling, and boring and immature, and weird and not-cute, and I pick at my skin and I can't even help it, and sometimes I'm mean. People like that don't deserve Bailey's friendship.*

"Yeah, I looked at your exhibition. You weren't always a perfect friend. I get it. So what?"

Vanessa blinked. *So what?*

"I wasn't talking about Bailey anyway," she lied.

"So if you're not inviting Bailey into the museum, who *are* you inviting?" asked Sterling.

Vanessa thought fast. "The twins. Rosalie and Honore."

"Cool," said Eli. "In that case, can I invite my friend Dan? He's the best. He's better at pranks than anyone I've ever met. I promise you, every day is April Fool's Day with Dan, and when it's *actually* April first? Ohhh boy, you better look out, take it from me. And double-check every bathroom before going in there."

Vanessa had a bad feeling about Dan. She waited for Sterling to add in his own crummy idea for someone else to join them, but he kept his mouth shut. She said, "We can't just invite *any* random person to join us. Then we'd be overrun with curators."

"I dunno, Rosalie and Honore sound pretty random to me," Eli said.

"You know what we need?" Vanessa said. "Rules."

Sterling caught her eye and mouthed *bossy.* Equally silently, Vanessa mouthed back *sexist.* She grabbed the permanent marker and a sheet of paper and wrote on it: *The Curators' Code.*

"Whenever Bailey and I started a club, we'd make a list of things that all members of the club had to agree to,"

Vanessa explained to the boys. "If you need an example, you can see the list of rules from our Gibby Giraffe Fan Club in display case 3A."

"Which one is display case 3A?" asked Sterling.

"That's what the map is for, remember?"

"Oh, right."

"Rules for being a curator," Vanessa said. "Number one: You have to contribute to the museum's collection in a meaningful way. I say you should have to present an application describing what your exhibition would be about, how much space you need, and which items you already have and which you'd still need to acquire. Then we can decide which applications to approve, so it'll only be people who are serious about this."

"*We* didn't have to do that," Eli pointed out.

"That's because we found the museum first."

"Fair enough," said Eli. "Okay, I have a rule, too. Rule the second: You have to be respectful of the other curators' exhibitions. Like you can't just move their displays around without their permission."

"Oh, that reminds me," Sterling said, "we should get some kind of security system to keep out trespassers and thieves."

"Do you really think we'd get thieves?" Eli asked, looking around the museum. "Who'd want to steal

Einstein's old water bowl? Someone with a really thirsty dog?'

"No one would be interested in stealing either of your junk," Sterling said to both Eli and Vanessa. "But other people collect baseball cards. And museum heists really do happen."

"That's true," said Vanessa. "Like at the Isabella Stewart Gardner Museum."

"What's that?" asked Eli.

"Oh, it's so cool," said Sterling.

"It's one of the most famous unsolved art heists," Vanessa explained. "More than thirty years ago, some thieves stole a bunch of famous works of art from this museum in Boston. They were never caught, and the artwork was never recovered. The museum has offered a *ten million dollar* reward for anyone who can help them solve the mystery."

"We went there on vacation a couple years ago," Sterling added. "They still have the empty frames up, to show you where the paintings are supposed to be."

"Whoa." Eli's mouth hung open.

"Okay," Vanessa said, "Rule three: We all have to do our part to keep the museum secure and the collection safe."

The boys nodded.

"Rule four is kind of like that, too," Vanessa said. "We all have to contribute to overall museum maintenance. Meaning everyone has to sweep up the leaves and trash that come in, and everyone has to dust the displays, and everyone has to tape up any labels that fall down."

"But I hate sweeping," Eli objected.

"*Everyone* hates sweeping," Vanessa said, and she wrote down the rule.

"Rule five," said Eli. "Something about keeping it a secret."

"Like, no telling adults?" suggested Vanessa, her marker hovering over the paper.

"Definitely no telling adults," Sterling agreed. "If Mom found out that we were hanging out in an abandoned museum, she'd freak. I bet she already knows some human-interest news story about kids who hung out in an abandoned museum and then all their teeth fell out or something."

"I have a question," Eli said. "If the rule is just not to tell adults, does that mean we *can* tell other kids? Can we give tours of the collection, like a real museum?"

Vanessa was torn. On the one hand, she was proud of what they'd created, and she wanted to show it off. She wanted it to be a *real* museum, where people could learn

and explore and discover. On the other hand, she was still worried about outsiders messing it up.

But what she wanted most was to show it to Bailey. So Bailey could see that she knew what she had done. And that she was sorry.

Vanessa chewed at the skin around her fingernails for a moment, then finally said, "Yes, we can let other kids in. *But* one of us has to be here any time there are any visitors, to supervise. And we can only invite people who will appreciate the museum. Kids who will get what it is, and not blab about it everywhere and get us in trouble."

Sterling and Eli both nodded. "Agreed."

"When can we have our first visitors?" Eli was wriggling with excitement, almost like he himself was a dog.

"Sunday after Hebrew school?" Vanessa suggested. "Let's say three o'clock."

Eli pumped his fist. "Sunday funday!"

"Sunday funday," Vanessa repeated, a smile spreading over her face.

She taped the Curators' Code to the inside of the admissions booth and admired it. It was good to have rules. She felt like they were prepared for anything.

Looking back, she couldn't have been more wrong.

CHAPTER 13

The museum's official opening day dawned wet, windy, and gray. It was a day for staying home in pajamas, drinking hot cocoa, and reading a book. It was *not* a day for waking up at eight A.M. to go to Hebrew school. Nor was it a day for museums.

Well, actually, it was a day for *some* museums—the ones with umbrella racks and windows that weren't broken. As Vanessa's mom drove the car to Hebrew school, she even asked, "If this rain keeps up, do you want to go to the museum this afternoon?"

"What?!" Vanessa yelled. How did her mother know? *How did her mother always know?!*

Her mom looked at her like she was nuts, then returned

her eyes to the road. "The children's museum," she clarified. "It's a good indoor activity."

"Oh right." Vanessa exhaled deeply. "That museum. No, thank you. I think . . . I'm too old for it now."

For some reason, this made Vanessa's mom look sad. "Is this because you got stuck in the climbing structure last time?"

"No." Vanessa looked out the window. "I just don't want to go there today, that's all."

Her mom pulled the car as close to the synagogue as possible. "If you see a clown carrying a computer today," she said, "steer clear."

"Okay," said Vanessa, climbing out of the car. "I will."

She ran fast, but even so she was mildly damp by the time she made it inside. The rain made her hair feel even bushier than usual.

"Hey," Eli whispered as she slid into the seat next to him. "Are you excited or what?"

"Yeah!" Vanessa said, but she couldn't tell whether the funny feeling inside her stomach really was excitement, or whether it was fear. She was scared that nobody would show up—because of the rain, or because it seemed boring, or because they found something better to do.

But she was also scared that people *would* show up, and that by seeing her museum exhibition they would be kind of seeing inside of her mind. So if they didn't like the exhibition, that would mean they didn't like *her*—like, as a person.

Maybe she should have made her exhibition less personal, more like Sterling's. Maybe they should delay the museum's grand opening until she had time to build a collection and display of something innocent, like stamps, or pencils.

Ms. Adler yelled *"Shechet b'vakasha!"* then. Class was starting. Vanessa and Eli both turned to face front.

Because Passover was just a couple weeks away, they were learning about the Jews' exodus from Egypt, where they'd been kept as slaves. This happened thousands and thousands of years ago, and there was a whole book in the Torah about it. Vanessa already knew the story, because they told it every year. But that was just the way religion was. You said the same prayers and read the same Torah portions and performed the same rituals week after week, year after year, generation after generation.

Vanessa found the repetition boring but also kind of miraculous, because it meant that she was doing the same

things her mother had when she was a kid, and her mother before her, and her mother's great-grandmother who'd been killed during the Holocaust, and back and back for as long as anyone could remember, maybe even way back to when the Jews were slaves in Egypt.

Vanessa sighed as she noticed that she had already torn a strand of skin off her ring finger. Fortunately, she had come prepared. She took a sheet of origami paper out of her bag and started folding a frog. She'd gotten pretty good at frogs.

"Who remembers where we left off on Thursday?" asked Ms. Adler.

Becky Felsenstein raised her hand immediately. "The Jews had escaped Egypt," she said, "and gotten through the Red Sea, and then they were wandering in the desert, and some other stuff happened, and they came to Mount Sinai, and Moses went up to the top of Mount Sinai to talk to God, and God—"

"That's where we stopped, Becky," Ms. Adler reminded her.

"I know, but I read ahead."

Ms. Adler took over from there. "Moses left the rest of the Jews at the base of the mountain, telling them to wait for him to get back. He climbed to the top of Mount Sinai—"

"Ms. Adler?" Eli waved his hand in the air. "I have a question. Why does 'Sinai' sound like 'sinus'? Like was the mountain shaped like a nose, or what?"

The teacher paused for a moment, clearly trying to decide whether to answer his question seriously or whether to tell him to shut it. "It's a coincidence," she finally replied.

"Oy gevalt," Eli exclaimed in a thick, fake Yiddish accent, clutching his head. "Such a pain I have in my Sinai!"

The class giggled. Ms. Adler ignored them and continued on with the story. "Moses climbed to the top of Mount Sinai, where God gave him the Ten Commandments on two stone tablets. Moses was up there for a total of forty days and forty nights."

"Forty days!" Eli said. "That's a long time. Where did he go to the bathroom?"

Eli was just being a brat, but this was actually a good question. It also made Vanessa wish they could get a working bathroom in the museum, but without running water and electricity, it wasn't possible. If you were at the museum and you had to pee, all you could do was hold it.

The origami actually seemed to be working so far. She hadn't picked at her skin since she'd started on this frog, even though this was a long time to sit still and listen.

Maybe *this* was the solution! Maybe Vanessa had finally found a way to fix whatever was wrong with her. Maybe she could do origami every day for weeks or months, however long it took for her hands to forget how good it felt to pick. And then she'd be cured. She'd be normal. Plus, she'd be the best origami-folder in the world.

Ms. Adler said, "Moses was gone for so long that the other Hebrews' faith began to break down. They weren't confident that they could trust in God because they had never seen Him. So they gathered all the women's jewelry and melted it all down to form an idol. Does anyone know what the idol depicted?"

"A—" Becky Felsenstein began.

"Anybody else?" Ms. Adler asked. "Literally anybody. Aaron! You look ready to answer a question. What do you think their idol was?"

"Um . . . Agollekaff," mumbled Aaron Silber.

"Could you say that again," Ms. Adler requested, "without the food in your mouth."

Everyone waited while Aaron chewed, swallowed, and then said more clearly, "A golden calf."

"Correct," Ms. Adler said. "By the way, you *are* aware that you're not allowed to eat snacks during class, yes?"

"Well, I had no way of knowing that you were going to call on me," Aaron said defensively.

"Kids," Ms. Adler said, sounding fed up. "You're a year away from your b'nai mitzvot, and yet you're acting like disrespectful children. Eating in class! Joking about toilets! Doing whatever it is that Vanessa is doing over there!"

Everyone in the class swiveled to look at Vanessa.

She turned bright red and dropped her hands into her lap.

"Vanessa, *what* are you doing in the middle of my class?" Ms. Adler asked.

Vanessa wanted to shrink into nothing. "Origami," she whispered.

"Origami?" Ms. Adler repeated.

Vanessa nodded silently.

Ms. Adler briefly closed her eyes. "Vanessa, is this art class?"

Vanessa shook her head.

"Oh?" Ms. Adler said. "Really? How interesting. What is it?"

"Hebrew school," Vanessa answered, her voice even smaller.

"And does this seem like an appropriate situation in which to be engaging in *origami*? Anybody?"

Vanessa bit her lip, trying not to cry.

Everyone shook their heads . . .

Except for Eli.

"Origami is a mitzvah," he called from the other side of the room.

Mitzvah was the Hebrew word for a good deed. Lots of things could be a mitzvah, like forgiveness or charity. Not origami, though.

"No, Eli—" Ms. Adler moved away from Vanessa and on toward him.

"Oh, you're right, you're right," Eli said. "It's one of the Ten Commandments, actually. I forgot."

"Eli—"

"That's why they made the golden calf, right? Because they didn't like the Ten Commandments?"

"No," Ms. Adler said, blessedly returning to the lesson. "The Jews waiting at the base of Mount Sinai for forty days had no way of knowing whether Moses would return. That's why they made the golden calf. So when Moses *did* return, he flew into a rage, and he broke the stone tablets given to him by God. Remember, the Ten Commandments *starts* with an order to worship only God: 'I am the Lord, your God, who brought you out of the land of Egypt, and

thou shalt have no other gods before me.' It's the very first rule of Judaism. And yet here were the Jewish people, worshipping a false god!"

Slowly, silently, trying not to attract any more attention to herself, Vanessa slid the brightly colored paper off her lap and placed it back in her bag, where no one could see it or ask about it or make fun of it.

"Can you think of any idols that you worship in your own lives?" asked Ms. Adler.

They all stared at her blankly. "We're Jewish," Miriam Rudolfsky reminded her.

"What about your phones?" Ms. Adler said, raising an eyebrow, like she'd caught them all in a lie.

"I don't *worship* my phone," said Sam Gordon.

Eli slipped out of his seat and onto his knees, lifting and lowering his arms as though in the throes of spiritual passion. "Oh, phone!" he cried out. "Phone, thou art good and great, beautiful and noble!" Other kids giggled, which only encouraged him. "Verizon Wireless, every day we sing your praises! Samsung, you give our lives meaning!"

"Eli," Ms. Adler snapped.

Eli returned to his chair and said in a normal tone of voice, "No, I don't think we think our phones are idols."

Vanessa realized she was already picking her cuticles again. So much for being the world's best origami folder. And so much for being cured.

Ms. Adler sighed deeply and pressed her fingers to her temples. "My point," she said after a moment, "is that we should resist the urge to imbue objects with more power or meaning than they actually have. The golden calf was not actually God. It was just a hunk of melted-down jewelry."

"Well, obviously," said Becky Felsenstein. "Everybody knows that."

CHAPTER 14

Inside the museum, the floor was damp, but the sound of falling rain was muffled. There wasn't much natural lighting today, but they'd arranged battery-powered lanterns and tea lights all around, so the artifacts were visible. The three of them—Vanessa, Sterling, and Eli—stood behind the admissions booth in the center of the room. And they waited.

"Well," said Vanessa.

Sterling coughed.

It was seven minutes past three.

"I know my cousin will come," Eli said, checking his phone.

"What makes you so sure?" asked Vanessa.

"I promised to give him shared custody of my best joke book if he showed up. *Nobody* would turn that down."

Sterling snorted but did not say anything.

"Who did you invite?" Vanessa asked her brother.

"Hayden." Hayden had been Sterling's friend back in elementary school.

"Who else?" Vanessa asked.

"Just Hayden."

"We said we would each invite two of our friends."

"Yeah, well, I only felt like inviting Hayden." And that was all Sterling would say on the matter.

Vanessa turned to Eli and said, "Hey, thanks for saving me from Ms. Adler today. That was nice of you."

Eli shrugged. "It was nothing."

"What did Ms. Adler do?" Sterling asked.

"Vanessa was fiddling with some paper or something and Adler got annoyed because nobody respects her, which by the way is not *our* fault. I'd respect her if there was anything to respect." Eli yawned. "What *were* you doing with that paper?"

"It's origami," Vanessa said. She paused, not wanting to give Eli the full answer. At last she just said, "I just wanted to keep my hands busy because sometimes I get bored."

"Me too," Eli said. "That's why I make jokes."

It was nice to know that she and Eli had this in common. Probably most people got bored, Vanessa thought. She just wished that her way of dealing with boredom wasn't so ugly.

When the clock showed thirteen minutes past three, Vanessa spoke. "Maybe we should try again next week—" But just then, the garbage bag over the window moved to the side. And the museum's first guests crawled inside.

"Sorry we're late," said Honore. "We had trouble figuring out where the entrance was."

"*This* is your museum?" Rosalie exclaimed, her eyes wide as she tried to take in the whole room. At first Vanessa couldn't tell if she meant that in a good way or a bad way, but then she continued: "It's amazing!"

Suddenly, Vanessa was able to see the museum through Rosalie's eyes. And her heart swelled. It *was* amazing.

"You can walk around and enjoy the exhibits," said Eli. "We'll be starting the next tour when everyone else shows up."

" 'The *next* tour'?" Sterling whispered.

"It makes it sound like we know what we're doing," Eli whispered back.

The next people to arrive were Sterling's friend Hayden and their little sister. "Hope it's okay that I brought along

MacKenzie," they said. "I know you told me to keep this place on the down-low, but I was babysitting and couldn't just leave her at home. Mac's a good secret-keeper, though—right, kid? Hey, whoa, this place is *dope*."

Then Eli's cousin showed up, as well as his friend—Dan, the known prankster. Vanessa kept her eye on him. Before inviting people to the museum's grand opening, they'd agreed to make it a small group, as sort of a practice round. But now that there were nine people in this space that just a few weeks ago had been so neglected and empty, it didn't feel small at all. It felt like something really big. Bigger than Vanessa ever could have imagined.

"Ahem!" Vanessa said after the guests all had time to explore a little on their own. "The next tour will be leaving from the admissions counter momentarily."

Their guests gathered around expectantly. "The tour begins in the Baseball Card Wing," said Sterling, leading them over there. "I will be your docent for this section of the tour. Here you can see the museum's collection of two hundred and thirty-one baseball cards, spanning back to the 1960s. Highlights of the collection include a signed card from Yasiel Puig, a near-mint condition Willie McCovey card, and Steven Kwan's rookie

card. You can see that the collection is arranged geographically, so here in the upper left-hand corner, for example, are six players for the Seattle Mariners. Particularly noteworthy is that we have the complete collection of rookie cards for the Cleveland team from 2017, 2018, and 2019."

Their dad felt that everyone should have a "home team" that they rooted for, which was why he gave Sterling so many baseball cards for the Cleveland team. Usually when he came to visit, he drove them to Progressive Field to watch a game. Vanessa enjoyed the snacks and the T-shirt cannon, but the game itself seemed to be long periods of time when nothing happened, interspersed with the occasional exciting thing that happened while Vanessa was looking someplace else.

The museum guests asked a few questions about the baseball cards, and Vanessa whispered, "What's a docent?"

"It's the person who shows guests around a museum," Sterling replied.

"Wow. Nice."

Sterling grinned. "I thought it'd make us sound professional."

"Now follow me," said Eli, "to the museum's Einstein Wing!"

"Einstein gets too much attention," commented Rosalie as Eli led the group to his display tables. "He wasn't even as good a scientist as Tesla."

"Well, this exhibition isn't about the scientist Einstein. It's about my dog Einstein. So you're in luck."

Rosalie grinned.

"Here you can see the bandana he sometimes wore around his neck. The groomer put it on him after one appointment and said, 'A handsome kerchief for a handsome boy.' Which was hilarious, because Einstein was really weird looking. After that we called Einstein 'handsome' all the time. Like, 'Hey, Handsome threw up on the rug again.' We don't have any of his throw up on display here, don't worry."

"He was super-weird looking," confirmed Eli's cousin.

"And here's a half-eaten bone," Eli went on. "He was working his way through it when he died. If he'd had another two months, he would've finished it off, no problem."

"How did he die?" asked Hayden.

"Kidney failure," said Eli.

Dan farted.

Vanessa was a little bit scared of big, slobbery dogs, but she found herself regretting that she'd never met Einstein in person. (In dog?) She felt like she knew him, sort of, from this exhibition. She found herself wondering: If you put together every item that touched Einstein—every toy and bowl and leash and vet report—would it be as good as having known him for real? Or would there always be something missing—some essential Einstein-ness that couldn't be captured in any amount of stuff?

After the Einstein Wing, their guests stopped in front of Maria's painting.

"Ooh, I'm digging this," said Hayden. "Who made it?"

"Maria." Sterling pointed at the signature.

"Who's Maria?" asked Hayden.

"No idea."

"She was good, whoever she was." Honore inspected the painting from all angles, her eyes wide. "Even our art teacher can't paint like this. You seriously just *found* this here?"

Vanessa nodded. "I wish I knew anything about it."

"Can I look at the back?" Honore asked. When Vanessa nodded, she edged the painting away from the wall that it was leaning against, just enough so she could crawl behind it. "Who's Richelle?" Her voice came out muffled.

"Who?" Vanessa asked.

Honore's popped her head out the far side. "On the back it says "For Richelle."

"Wait, what?" Vanessa immediately dropped to her knees and joined Honore behind the artwork. Honore held up her phone's flashlight to shed light on the back of the frame. There, in small, faint letters, as promised, the words *FOR RICHELLE* were printed.

Vanessa couldn't believe that in all the time she'd spent wondering about this mystery painting, it had never occurred to her to study the *back* of it. Now she scanned the thick wood frame all over, looking for any other clue, but those two words were all she could find.

"Is that the same handwriting as the artist's signature?" Honore asked. "So Maria painted this as a gift for Richelle?"

"I think you're right!" Vanessa said.

"Are you guys ever coming out?" came Eli's voice. "Our guests are getting bored."

"I'm not bored," Rosalie's voice said. Vanessa and Honore crawled back out anyway. Vanessa looked at the painting in a new light. Was one of the people in it Maria? Was the other Richelle?

"I bet you could get it appraised," Honore said. "Maybe it's worth something."

"I doubt it," Sterling said. "If it was worth anything, why would it have gotten left behind in a closed-down museum?"

"Plus," Eli said, "I think if a crew of kids showed up at some art appraiser's office with a giant painting that they didn't know anything about, the appraiser would probably have some questions."

They all stood at the painting for a few minutes longer, making guesses about who Maria might have been, why she might have painted this piece, and how it got left there. It was weird to think that they might never know. They could tell whatever stories they wanted, and no one could ever disprove them.

And then it was time. They moved on to the next and final stop of the tour:

The Bailey Wing.

Vanessa stood beside the first display case and tore at the skin around her fingernails. Everyone else gathered around in a semicircle. "A lot of museums are about history," she began. "They have items that show you how people used to live and what they used to care about. Like, 'Here's a contraption that the prince of Denmark used to clean his teeth in the 1200s.'"

Eli laughed a little, which gave Vanessa courage.

"This museum exhibit is like that, too, only it's not about the 1200s. It's about very recent history. It's about how people used to live and what they used to care about just a

few weeks or months ago. And by 'people,' I mean my best friend, Bailey Dominguez. I know Bailey's not the prince of Denmark. But she's way more important to me than any famous celebrity or historical figure could ever be. And I . . . I messed up. I drove her away."

Vanessa took them through the whole exhibit: the watercolor of a sunset that Bailey had painted; the board game that the two of them had created together, called Veggieland (like Candy Land, only without candy); Vanessa's half of the two-headed monster that had been their Halloween costume in fifth grade; and all the rest of it. As she spoke, Vanessa pretended that Bailey was one of the people on this tour. That she was showing Bailey how important their friendship was and how sorry she was.

But when she got to the dress, and how horrible she had been to Bailey, Rosalie spoke up.

"That's not how it happened."

Everyone, including Vanessa, turned to her. "What do you mean?" Vanessa asked.

"Just what I said. We were there, and that wasn't what happened. Right, Honore?"

Rosalie's sister nodded. "It's *sort of* what happened, but you left out everything she said about your dad."

Vanessa felt like the ground was tilting beneath her.

"What did Bailey say about our dad?" Sterling asked. Vanessa could see his hand curling into a fist.

"Let's see." Rosalie closed her eyes briefly, like she was conjuring the memory. "We were doing a fashion show. It was the four of us plus Salima, and we'd all brought over some of our best outfits and we made a playlist and we were using Bailey's upstairs hallway as our catwalk."

Vanessa could picture the scene clearly. She'd spent so much of her life in Bailey's upstairs hallway, she knew every inch of it by heart.

"Salima was complaining about having Katarina as her social studies partner," Honore went on. To the rest of the group, she explained, "Katarina was a girl in our fifth-grade class who always got *terrible* grades. Nobody wanted to work with her."

"And Bailey said that the reason why Katarina did so poorly in school was because her dad wasn't around."

Vanessa felt too cold and too hot all at the same time—the same way she had when this actually happened.

Rosalie kept talking. "And Vanessa said, 'What does her dad not being around have to do with her getting bad grades?' And Bailey was like, 'Well, it's not that *I* think there's a connection. It's just that my *dad* says there's a connection. There are all these articles and studies about

it. Kids without dads do worse in school. They can't help it. It's just, like, science.'"

Vanessa remembered all this now. How awkward it had been, because everyone knew that Vanessa's dad lived thousands of miles away, but Bailey was pretending like she was still talking about Katarina or just some objective *science*, and not her best friend who was actually in the hallway right there with her. How Vanessa herself had been struggling in school, because she just couldn't wrap her mind around long division, and how it felt like Bailey was blaming her or her dad for it.

"And Bailey was like, 'Poor Katarina, I don't see how she's going to survive middle school,'" Vanessa recalled. "'She can't keep getting away with this next year.'"

Vanessa remembered how enraged and powerless she felt. She knew that Bailey was actually talking about her. *Everybody* knew Bailey was talking about her. But, because she was *technically* talking about Katarina, it felt like there was nothing Vanessa could say in her own defense.

"And *that's* when I told her she'd gotten too big to ever fit into her communion dress again," Vanessa said.

The twins nodded. "I mean, you definitely shouldn't have said that," Honore said, looking at the dress. "But

she shouldn't have said all that stuff about your grades and your dad, either."

"You're absolutely right she shouldn't have," Sterling said. His eyes flashed with fury. "I knew I should've kicked her butt."

"And *I* knew she's the worst," Eli added.

And, while the day was as rainy and dark as ever, Vanessa felt suddenly as though a beam of light was shining straight down on her. Freedom had finally come. *None of this was her fault.* The truth was this: Bailey was a bad friend, and she was fortunate to be rid of her.

CHAPTER 15

After that, the museum got bigger and better with each passing day.

A few of Vanessa's classmates approached her in homeroom on Tuesday morning. "Can we see it?" asked Sydney.

"See what?" said Vanessa, setting down her origami paper.

"You know." Sydney lowered her voice. "The secret museum."

"Oh!" Vanessa was flattered.

"Honore told me about it," said Chloe. "She said it was a *real* museum. She said it was the coolest thing she'd ever seen, except for the time when she went to Disney World. She said it was less cool than Disney World."

"It's a *little* less cool than Disney World," Vanessa conceded.

"So when can we come?" asked Beckett.

Vanessa hadn't discussed with Eli and Sterling when they would next open the museum. "How about after school tomorrow?" she suggested, and the girls agreed. "But before you can come, you need to know that there are a few rules." She dropped her voice, and they leaned in to hear. "Most important, no telling any adults. If you need your parents to drive you over, just tell them that we're going to play in the park. If you *do* slip up and mention the museum, just pretend like it's some small thing in my bedroom that I'm calling a museum, like for make-believe. They'll buy that."

The three girls nodded seriously.

Vanessa caught Bailey watching them from across the room. Did she look curious? Maybe even . . . jealous?

Vanessa hoped she'd be jealous or curious enough to come visit the museum herself. To see the exhibits and to feel the guilt that she deserved. Vanessa was once again rewriting the labels—this time so that everyone

would know what a bad friend and bad person Bailey was. It was surprising, once she got started, how much she could find, how many stories and examples of the badness of Bailey.

ITEM #19: TWO-HEADED MONSTER HALLOWEEN COSTUME

Materials: Fur, googly eyes, a leotard, some other stuff. Bailey and I always liked to do our Halloween costumes together. We spent a long time creating this two-headed monster, but at the very last minute Bailey decided she didn't want to wear it to school after all. I had to wear my half on my own. So I was just a one-headed monster all day, because Bailey bailed on me.

ITEM #8: THE DAYS ARE JUST PACKED: A CALVIN AND HOBBES COLLECTION, BY BILL WATTERSON

Materials: paper.
One time Bailey "borrowed" this book from my mom's bookshelf for like two years. (aka, she stole it.) She never even returned it—one time I was over at her house and saw it on her desk so I just took it back. If I hadn't done that, it would still be there.

The girls from homeroom were the first to ask to see the museum, but many others soon followed. Word spread quickly—through Vanessa's and Eli's schools, through Temple Beth Elohim, through the neighborhood pick-up games of tag and kickball. So many kids wanted to visit the museum that Vanessa created an official schedule. Now, when people asked, she told them that the museum was open from two to four P.M. on Saturdays and Sundays, and for two hours after school on Wednesdays. During those times, Vanessa was there to greet guests, show them around, and answer their questions. Usually the other curators joined her.

Maria's painting was usually the most popular part, which made sense, because it was beautiful and

mysterious. Everyone who visited asked where it had come from and who made it and what it meant—so much so that Vanessa made a label for it that said in big letters WE DON'T KNOW.

Vanessa told Honore and Rosalie that they could apply to curate their own exhibit, so they did. Vanessa had assumed they'd want to do one together and was surprised when they handed in two completely different proposals. (Dan, thankfully, never bothered to put together a proper application for his idea, an exhibit on the history of boogers.)

Rosalie's was a science and technology exhibit. She brought over a crate of wires and batteries and made a label carefully explaining how electrical circuits work. She made and hung a papier-mâché model of the solar system. She even built an interactive chute that museum visitors could send marbles down, to see how the angle of the slide affected the marble's velocity. "I get bored at museums where all you can do is look at things," she explained. "People should be able to *do* stuff, too."

Honore put up an art exhibit. She hung her watercolors and drawings in the museum's empty frames and wrote labels explaining her "technique" and "intent." It made

Vanessa wish all the more that they knew the truth about the Maria's painting, whose label looked so bare next to Honore's.

So many visitors came to the museum that Eli said they should start charging an admission fee. "Look, I have a lot of expenses."

"Like what?" Sterling scoffed.

"Like whoopee cushions," Eli said.

"Exactly how much money are you spending on whoopee cushions?" asked Sterling.

Eli shook his head. "You don't even want to know."

They settled on a two-dollar admission for everyone over the age of six, and free for anyone younger. "That way," Vanessa reasoned, "if someone has to babysit a younger sibling, they can still come to the museum without having to buy two tickets."

"What if people *pretend* to be six years old so they can get in for free?" asked Sterling.

"No one's going to do that," said Eli.

"Mom still has me pretend to be twelve so she can buy me a children's ticket at the movies," Sterling replied.

"Your mom's a lawbreaker," said Eli.

"Paying full price at the movies isn't a law," Sterling said.

"We know how old most of the people coming really are," said Vanessa. "It's not like they're total strangers."

Sterling admitted that this was a good point.

So they hung a sign with the museum's hours and admission price, and they put the money in an old jewelry box of Vanessa's. Some of the money they divvied up equally, so Eli could buy his whoopee cushions and the rest of them could buy whatever they wanted. (Maybe more origami paper. Vanessa was going through it at a fast clip.)

But the majority of the proceeds went to museum expenses. Honore drew a map of the museum on paper and they made photocopies. They bought stickers and gave them to guests to wear at the museum, to show that they'd paid admission. They bought more lamps and batteries so all the displays could be clearly lit—including the side rooms, which they were expanding into as the number of exhibits grew. Running a museum wasn't free.

There was also the cost of building a security system. Sterling was insistent that they needed one to protect his baseball cards. Rosalie was insistent that they needed one because installing a security system sounded cool.

Rosalie made their security system with a complicated setup of magnets, sensors, rope, and a hidden cell

phone. When anyone pulled on the bag covering the window entryway, it tugged on a rope, which then activated a magnet, which pushed a button on the phone, which called Vanessa. That way Vanessa would know if someone was breaking into the museum.

"How do you just randomly have an extra phone?" Sterling asked. "I had to beg my mom to get me even *one* phone."

"Everyone in my family gives me their broken old electronics when they upgrade," Rosalie explained. "So I can do projects with them."

"You're a genius," Eli told Rosalie. "You're like Einstein. The real one. Not my dog."

"I told you, Einstein is overrated," Rosalie said. "I'd rather be like Tesla." She kept opening and closing the window covering, and Vanessa's phone kept ringing.

The security system didn't work a hundred percent of the time. If you knew it was there, you could slide yourself sideways through the window without setting it off. But it was good enough to catch most ordinary would-be thieves.

During the museum's opening hours, they kept the window covering pinned to the side so that Vanessa's phone wouldn't be constantly ringing. They always had a steady stream of guests. Some people just came once, but a lot

of them came back, bringing new friends with them and excitedly showing them around the museum as though *they* were the experts. Vanessa and her friends gave tour after tour until they'd all memorized one another's talks.

It was the best thing ever, but it wasn't always perfect. One day, Vanessa was perched on the admissions booth when she heard an "eek!" immediately followed by a *crash*. Vanessa hopped off the booth and ran over to the girl who stood in the Bailey Wing, her hands covering her mouth.

"I am *so* sorry," the girl blurted out.

"It's okay," Vanessa said automatically, before realizing that she didn't actually know if it was okay because she didn't know what had happened.

"I was just turning around to look for my friend," the girl explained, "and my elbow knocked into the bowl on that pedestal. It fell to the ground before I could do anything. It was a total accident."

Vanessa knelt to pick up the pieces of the clay bowl that the girl was referring to. Bailey had made it in pottery. She'd carved her initials into the bottom so that it wouldn't get confused with anyone else's bowls in the kiln. Vanessa turned the pieces over now. One had the letter *B* on it. The other had most of the letter *D*. They didn't quite fit together. A shard must have flown off somewhere.

"I am *such* a klutz," the girl went on. "Maybe I can buy you a replacement? Where did you get it?"

Vanessa held a piece in each hand. If the girl had read the label, she would know that was a dumb question.

"Is there anything I can do?" The girl looked like she might cry.

"It's okay," Vanessa said, and this time she meant it. Or at least she really, really tried to. What did it matter if Bailey's one-of-a-kind bowl got destroyed? If Bailey was a bad friend—and she *was*—then why should Vanessa care? "It was an accident. Accidents happen."

She thought about how long it had taken Bailey to make this bowl. To knead the clay, and throw it on the potter's wheel, to shape it and sculpt it, to let it dry, to fire it, to glaze it, to do all the other steps that Vanessa was now forgetting. Bailey had described the whole process once. It took a long time to make, but to ruin it took almost no effort at all.

Vanessa put the pieces of the bowl in the trash bag that they now kept by the entryway. Even she was not so pathetic or nostalgic as to hang on to a bowl that wasn't a bowl anymore.

"It's the cost of doing business," Sterling reassured her. "You know, like the art heist at the Isabella Stewart

Gardner Museum. If you put things on display, most of them will get preserved, and a couple of them will get ruined. It could've happened just the same if you'd kept the bowl at home."

Sterling had a point. Nowhere was ever truly safe.

Vanessa surveyed the rest of her Bailey display. It was so expansive; you wouldn't even notice that a single bowl was missing. She still had what was probably the best Bailey collection in the world.

"If this is the worst thing that happens at the museum," she said to Eli, "that's not bad."

Unfortunately, they discovered soon, the broken bowl was not the worst thing to happen at the museum. Not even close.

CHAPTER 16

Vanessa's dad arrived in town the week before Passover. The whole family went to pick him up at the airport. They held up a handwritten sign that said his name and had an American flag. Vanessa liked the sign because it seemed like a nice way to welcome someone, and also, secretly, because it guaranteed that her father would find them. Of course he knew what they looked like; they did video calls all the time, plus he'd just seen them in person last summer, and nobody grew *that* quickly. Still, she had some irrational fear that one day her dad wouldn't recognize her, or she wouldn't recognize him.

That didn't happen, though. Vanessa spotted her dad the instant he emerged from customs. He was wearing jeans and a pullover and carrying a backpack that was as big as a person.

"Daddy!" Vanessa called out, and Sterling shouted, "Dad!" and their father's eyes lit up as he jogged toward them. He gave them both huge hugs and kisses on the cheek. Vanessa closed her eyes and breathed in deep as she pressed her face to her father's chest. She heard his voice and saw his face all the time, but there was always something missing. She couldn't smell him through the computer. He smelled the same as he always did. She hoped that never changed.

It was only midday by the time they got home, but because of the time difference, their dad had already been up for more than sixteen hours. He wanted to shower and nap, but first Sterling wanted to show off his redecorated bedroom and Vanessa wanted to demonstrate the new trick she could do on the swing set and Sterling wanted to play him his new favorite song and Vanessa wanted to show him the T-shirt she'd tie-dyed, and he was practically falling asleep on his feet by the time their mom firmly closed him into the guest room and told Vanessa and Sterling to give him a break.

"I want to show him the museum," Vanessa whispered to Sterling.

"We can't," Sterling said. "Rule number five, remember?"

"I know." If they showed their dad the museum, he would have the same issues with it that any other grown-up would have. (This is illegal/dangerous/bad for some reason that only an adult would ever think of/etc.) And he would tell their mom, no question—even though they were separated, they still told each other everything when it came to Vanessa and Sterling. "I know we can't tell him," Vanessa said. "I'm just saying that I want to, that's all."

In fact, for the next week, Vanessa and her brother spent almost no time at the museum. They were too busy spending every possible second with their father. Instead of the museum, they went to the movies and to dinner and to mini-golf, even though it was raining, because their dad really wanted to play mini-golf with them.

They went to the Home Depot and spent like a hundred years there while their dad picked out a new toilet seat because he said their upstairs toilet slammed and he couldn't leave them with a slamming toilet. ("How long has this been going on for?" he asked them seriously. "I literally never noticed it before," answered Vanessa. Though she did notice the absence of a slam after he fixed it.)

They went to the bookstore and the candy store and he tried to get them to go to the bicycle store but Vanessa

put her foot down, because the bike shop was in the same shopping plaza as Pancho's and she wasn't going anywhere near Bailey's family's restaurant if she could help it.

Actually, Vanessa might have said no to a lot of these excursions if she'd felt like she had the option. She knew they were all technically fun things (except for the Home Depot trip, though even that *might* have been fun if it hadn't taken one hundred years). But they would have felt more fun if she'd had a choice in the matter, or if any of them had been her idea. Sometimes she didn't want to do anything especially fun. Sometimes she just wanted to sit around and watch videos on her phone. But she couldn't say that to her dad. He was only here for ten days. He'd come all this way just to spend time with her. She had to make it worth his while.

If Vanessa had thought there might be any time to stop by the museum over the weekend, she could think again, because Saturday was the day before Passover—two days before their dad was leaving—and their mom put everyone to work readying the house for the holiday.

And so began the annual process of putting extra leaves in the dining room table, bringing up folding tables from the basement, wiping them all down, ironing the nice linens which had sat in a box all year, laying out the

tablecloths, polishing the silverware and candlesticks, making place cards, arranging chairs. Plus there was all the prep for the seder plate: hard-boiling an egg, slicing celery, chopping up apple after apple to make haroset (Vanessa's favorite Passover food).

Once this was done, Sterling and Vanessa did the annual hunt for chametz, which was the only type of cleaning Vanessa actually enjoyed. Chametz was the Hebrew word for bread products, which you weren't allowed to eat during the eight days of Passover. That meant no cookies, no pasta, no pizza, no pretzels, and no bagels—which accounted for about eighty-five percent of everything Vanessa ate.

Not only could you not eat chametz, the tradition was that you couldn't even keep it in the house. Their mom boxed up all their flour and breakfast cereal and "sold" it to their non-Jewish next-door neighbor, Mr. Phillips. (He gave them a penny, and then he kept the box in his closet for the next eight days until they were ready to pick it up.) They were supposed to make sure that not even a crumb remained, and the traditional way to do this was to go through the house with only a candle for seeing chametz, a feather to scoop it up, and a wooden spoon to scoop it into.

Vanessa knew her mom purposefully placed big bread crumbs around the living room just to make sure they'd have something to find. She also knew that her mom would come through with a broom, vacuum, and mop at least twice before tomorrow's seder actually began, so the pressure on her to find chametz by candlelight was pretty low.

"Always hold on to the banister when you go down stairs," their mom told them as they searched.

"Okay," said Vanessa and Sterling. "We will."

"Why?" asked their dad.

Vanessa and Sterling rolled their eyes at each other. Their dad was not around enough to know that when their mom dispensed random wisdom gleaned from disturbing "human interest" stories, you should always agree with it and never request more information.

"Well," their mom explained eagerly, "there was this boy whose mother was cleaning the house for Passover. He was downstairs, but she needed to clean downstairs, so she chased him upstairs. Then he was upstairs, but she needed to clean upstairs, so she chased him downstairs. Then he was downstairs, but she needed to clean downstairs, so—"

"Let me guess," Sterling interrupted, "she chased him upstairs."

Their mother nodded brightly. "And then he fell down the stairs and died."

"*What?*" Sterling's and Vanessa's mouths hung open.

Their dad laughed. "Is that true?"

Their mom shrugged. "Either it's true or it's a story my great-aunt once told me. Could go either way."

Vanessa shook her head. *Some* mothers' stories had morals like "don't lie" or "apologize when you're wrong." *Her* mother's stories had morals like "hold on to the banister so your mom doesn't accidentally kill you while she's cleaning the house."

"This feels like a hint," their dad said. "I think somebody wants us out of the house for a bit. Kids, grab your sweaters. I have a surprise for you."

Their mom smiled and nodded, and so Vanessa and Sterling went.

The surprise was tickets to a Cleveland Guardians game. This was hardly a "surprise," since Vanessa totally guessed it as soon as they got in the car. Plus, when you had a surprise for somebody, it should be something *they* wanted, not something *you* wanted.

But her dad seemed delighted with the surprise, so she and Sterling played along.

They found their seats and then stood for the national anthem. Their dad got hot dogs from one of the vendors, and when he showed his military I.D. to purchase a beer, they gave him a free box of Cracker Jack, too.

"This is as good as it gets," their dad told them, resting an arm around each of their shoulders. "A beautiful spring evening with my two favorite people in the world, watching this great nation's greatest sports team. What a life."

"Plus we can still eat bread for another twenty-four hours," Sterling said, gesturing to his hot dog bun.

"That's right," their dad agreed. "Carbo-load while you can."

He heaved a deep, contented sigh, and Vanessa had to agree. Her dad was home and happy, and this was as good as it gets. She leaned her head against his shoulder.

He glanced down at her and drew his mouth into an exaggerated frown. "Honey, please stop picking at your cuticles."

"Sorry." Vanessa balled her hands into fists. This was only the millionth time her dad had said this to her in the past week.

The baseball players weren't doing anything interesting (*As usual*, Vanessa thought), so the big screen showed a gaggle of young women with long eyelashes and baseball caps. They laughed and pointed and waved at the camera.

"They're pretty cute, huh?" Vanessa's dad said, nudging Sterling.

"Ew, Dad. Gross," Vanessa replied. She was fine with the idea of her parents dating people, but that didn't mean she was okay with her dad commenting on the looks of girls who were half his age and were probably just trying to lead their lives without strangers voicing opinions on their cuteness. "Stop objectifying women," Vanessa added, which was something her mom said a lot.

"Good note," their dad said. "But Sterling, they looked like nice girls, am I right?"

The game had apparently started back up again (though how anyone could tell was beyond Vanessa), so the screen had gone back to showing the field. "I dunno," Sterling said, looking about as uncomfortable and annoyed as Vanessa felt when her dad told her to stop picking her skin. "They weren't really on the screen for that long. I didn't notice them."

"Any girls at school catch your eye?" their dad asked.

"No." Sterling's face was turning redder and redder.

"Any boys?"

Sterling shook his head.

"Well." Their dad patted Sterling's shoulder. "That's all right. It'll happen."

Vanessa chewed at the skin around her fingernails.

"What about your friends?" their dad pressed on. "Are any of them dating yet?"

"No."

"Any of them crushing on anybody? Is that still a phrase kids use? 'Crushing on'?"

"Dad," Sterling said, "I really don't want to talk about this with you."

"It's a natural part of growing up, Sterling," their father said. As though Sterling was doing something wrong, not growing up naturally. "Oh, hey, look alive, Jackson's up!"

The distraction couldn't have come at a better time. The next Guardians player stepped up to the plate, swung his bat a few times to warm up his arms, and got into his batting stance.

The pitcher wound up and tossed the ball.

"It's a fast one," Vanessa's dad narrated. "He's got this—"

Crack!

The ball went arcing into the air, and the batter dropped his bat and took off for first base.

"Yeah!" Vanessa's dad cheered. "Yeah! That's the stuff! Come on!" He leapt to his feet and pumped his fist as the Guardians player rounded first base, then second, and then—

"OUT!" called the umpire.

A player way out in the far left field had caught the ball on its way down. The home crowd groaned. The batter spat at the ground and jogged back to the dugout, his helmet pulled down low over his face.

Vanessa's dad sat back down and looked at her. "Hey," he said, "I have an idea for how you can stop picking at your cuticles."

Vanessa's shoulders tensed up. She hadn't *asked* for ideas for how she could stop picking.

"You know how some families have a swear jar?" her dad went on. "And every time someone swears, they have to put a quarter in the swear jar? We could do that for you. Every time you tear off your skin, you have to put a quarter in the jar."

Vanessa's mouth fell open. She stared at her father, speechless.

"That would motivate you to stop," her dad explained.

Like the problem was that she wasn't motivated!

"I don't like that idea," Vanessa mumbled.

"Okay, well, then we need another solution. What's *your* plan to quit"—he waved his hands at hers—"doing that to yourself?"

Vanessa looked down and tried to find a safe place for her hands. "I do origami," she reminded him.

"But that hasn't really solved anything, has it? You know, I honestly think attaching a little financial incentive could really change your—"

Something inside Vanessa snapped. "I ALREADY SAID I WAS SORRY!" she yelled.

Her dad recoiled. Sterling flinched and stared hard at the game, like he was absolutely fascinated.

"I *know* you want me to stop picking at my cuticles! I heard you the first million times! Why do you keep telling me?"

"Baby, it just makes me sad to see you hurt yourself," her dad said.

"I'M NOT DOING IT ON PURPOSE!" Vanessa roared, even though she felt like this must be untrue; surely she *was* doing it on purpose, because if not, then why was she doing it? "And I'm not doing it to make you sad!"

"Why are you yelling at me?" her dad asked, sounding utterly bewildered. "I'm trying to help you."

"You can't . . . you can't just show up once a year and think you can fix everything!"

People in the nearby seats were watching them and whispering.

"And you can't tell me what to do," Vanessa added, slightly quieter so that people would stop staring.

"Actually," her father said, "if I see you engaging in behavior that's destructive to yourself or to others, it is my *job*, as a parent who loves you, to tell you what to do."

"Mom doesn't care, though. *She's* fine with it. Are you saying she doesn't love me?" Vanessa challenged him.

Her dad frowned at her. "Your mom cares about you more than anything in the world. She doesn't want to see you mutilating your body any more than I do. Maybe she lets you get away with this sort of behavior a little more frequently than I would, but that doesn't mean she accepts it.

"Look, I know about discipline. Discipline is what I *do*. I've trained myself and my soldiers to do all sorts of hard things. But you've got to be willing to work for it. You have to *try*, Vanessa."

Vanessa didn't say a word. Not then, and not at all for the rest of the game. Not even when the Guardians won.

She curled up her leg under her and picked at the dry skin on her ankle and silently dared her father to try and stop her.

It was the same thing, over and over. Bailey. Her parents. Everyone wanted her to be somebody different. Because there was something wrong with her just the way she was.

CHAPTER 17

Vanessa was still in a crummy mood the next day, but she didn't have time to wallow because there was so much seder preparation to be done. She helped her mom make the matzah ball soup, forming the matzah meal into light little balls and carefully dropping them into the pot of boiling water to watch them pouf out. She opened the plastic packages of chocolate-covered marshmallows and macaroons and brightly colored fake fruit slices and arranged them on trays. She scooped horseradish out of a jar and onto the seder plate. She filled bowls with water and salt. She cut flowers. She placed a Haggadah—the Passover prayer book—on each seat. She cleaned her room, for no apparent reason, because no one was going to come upstairs during the seder, but her mother told her to clean so that was that. She showered and put on a navy-blue dress and her Star of David necklace. She looked in the mirror and thought that she almost might even look cute.

Guests started arriving just before six, bearing platters of chametz-free food and bottles of wine. There was Vanessa and Sterling's grandmother, who complained about everything. There was her mom's colleague from the news station, Mr. Manushkin, and his husband, Dr. Manushkin, who were dairy-free and sugar-free and gave Vanessa's mom weeks of anxiety about her menu. There was her mom's best friend, Lizzie; her husband, Dan; and the baby they had recently adopted. There was Jake, the twenty-three-year-old son of her mom's friend in Hawai'i, and Shelley, Jake's girlfriend, who only wanted to talk about Israel. There were a lot of people in the house, but none of them were kids who Vanessa could play with. (Unless you counted the baby, which she didn't.)

"Greetings, Edgar," Vanessa's grandmother said to Vanessa's father—literally, she used the word *greetings*, as though she was an alien. "How's the war going? I'm so glad you could make it home to spend this holiday with our family."

Vanessa caught her brother's gaze across the room and they exchanged a look. Vanessa's grandmother made no secret of disliking their father, to the point that she seemed to relish when he did something wrong and seemed disappointed when he did something right—like come home for a holiday. Today was maybe the first time ever that Vanessa was on her grandmother's side. Maybe it would have been better if he hadn't come.

"What war are you in?" asked Jake, polite but confused.

"At the moment, none, thankfully," Vanessa's dad said. "I'm a lieutenant colonel in the army, based in Ramstein, though I'm about to ship out to East Africa."

"Thank you for your service," said Dr. Manushkin, which was an appropriate thing to say to people in the armed forces. (Asking them "how's the war going?" was not appropriate.)

"How long are you in town for?" asked Dan.

"I leave tomorrow," said Vanessa's dad, "but I've been here for ten days."

"And what's been the best part of your visit?" Lizzie asked.

"Seeing the Guardians win a home game," Dad replied. "No question."

"Hey!" Sterling objected.

"Oh, that's right. And spending time with my beautiful children. I knew I'd forgotten something."

Everyone laughed, except for Vanessa's grandmother, who glowered. Even Vanessa laughed a little before she remembered she was too mad to laugh. Before she remembered that her dad didn't even really think she was beautiful.

They were seated at the long table that started in the dining room and continued all the way into the living room, with Vanessa and Sterling at one end and their mom closest to the kitchen. She started the seder with the blessings over the candles and the wine.

"Hey, man, pour me a glass of wine," Sterling said to Jake, like they were bros.

"You're fourteen," Vanessa said, and she passed him the grape juice that was on the table just for them.

Sterling made a face at her. "Dad, can I have wine?"

"No," their mom said.

"I was asking Dad."

Their grandmother looked at their father. Their father looked at their mother. The guests all looked at their wineglasses.

"This is your mother's house," their dad said at last. "Respect her rules."

"Okay, but if it were your house—"

"The answer is no, Sterling." Dad frowned at him, and the seder continued.

Their grandmother also frowned, because Dad had once again given a good answer.

Next up was the Four Questions, a Hebrew song that Vanessa always recited because traditionally it was sung by the youngest person at the seder table, and that was Vanessa.

"I used to do the Four Questions at my family's seder," said Jake, sounding very proud and relieved that he was by no means the youngest person at this table.

"And someday *you'll* do the Four Questions!" Lizzie cooed at her baby.

Vanessa didn't mind being the youngest every year. It made her feel important.

Every seder was essentially the same, not just in the Lepp household, but in homes all over the world, for all time. Of course each seder was unique—different foods, different people, different locations—but they all followed the same order. That was even what the word *seder* meant in Hebrew: order. That was part of what Vanessa liked about it. But also part of what made it boring.

And when Vanessa got bored, she picked at her skin. And picked. And picked. And there was a loooong time for boredom between the Four Questions and the next fun part (a song called "Dayenu"). When Vanessa noticed she was picking, she stuck her hands under her thighs so she'd stop. But then she'd get bored again and her hands would come back out.

And anyway, *so what*? Whose business was it but hers if her cuticles were raw and red and ragged? What made her parents think they could be in charge of everything about her? What made her dad think he had any idea how to fix her?

I'm hungry, Sterling texted Vanessa under the table.

Me too. Vanessa counted how many pages were left in the Haggadah before they could eat. Too many.

Finally they got to the Ten Plagues, which was the bit where everyone spilled out a drop of wine (or grape juice) for each plague that had been visited upon the ancient Egyptians. One for boils. One for hail. One for locusts. One for the death of each firstborn child, which honestly seemed like overkill but what did Vanessa know.

"Aren't we going to recite the plagues in Hebrew?" Vanessa's grandmother interrupted.

Vanessa's mom forced a closed-mouth smile. "Not everyone here reads Hebrew, Mom."

"Vanessa and Sterling should, by this point," their grandmother said. "You do, don't you? Vanessa's nearly a bat mitzvah, so if she can't read the Ten Plagues in Hebrew, she has some catching up to do. I'm sure everyone here *must* read at least basic Hebrew."

Jake and Shelley, having never been to the Lepp house before, looked confused. Lizzie and Dan, knowing exactly what was going on, looked uncomfortable.

Why is Grandma always so mean to Dad? Vanessa texted Sterling.

idk. Because he left Mom?

Mom left him. And anyway she was mean to him even when they were together.

Maybe because he's not Jewish?

So what? Lots of people aren't Jewish.

I dunno. Go ahead and ask her.

Vanessa squinted down the table toward her grandmother, who was now using an ice cube to scrub at a minuscule stain on the tablecloth.

No way, she texted back.

Their father came over and placed a hand on both their shoulders as their mom turned to the next page in the Haggadah. "No phones during seder," he reminded them under his breath.

"But Dad—" Sterling began.

"Do I need to hold on to them until the end of the night?"

That shut Sterling right up. They put their phones away and, with empty hands once again, Vanessa went back to picking. Her hands were under the table. Her dad couldn't see them anyway.

Finally it was time to eat. Everyone complimented the fluffiness of the matzah balls that Vanessa had made. For the first time in twelve months, Vanessa bit into matzah—the dry, flat, crumbly bread replacement that they ate during Passover and no other time of year. Vanessa had heard some people claim that they liked the taste of matzah. But she'd never heard that from anyone who actually *had* to eat it for eight days straight.

They feasted until they were stuffed, on salad and salmon and tzimmes and kugel and brisket, and some

people ate gefilte fish (but not Vanessa, because it was slimy and lumpy and gross). Mr. Manushkin and Vanessa's mom tried to one-up each other with crazy human interest stories. Lizzie and Dan told everyone about the call they got when their baby was ready for them, and how they hadn't known when to expect it so Dan had to run out in the middle of the night to buy diapers. Shelley tried unsuccessfully to steer the conversation toward Israel.

Then Vanessa's phone buzzed. Somebody was calling her.

Who would call during Passover?

Everyone was so engaged in eating and talking that they didn't pay attention when Vanessa slipped into the hallway to answer her phone. "Hello?" she said.

She was met with only silence.

"Hello?"

She pulled the phone away from her ear and looked at it.

Caller: Museum Security System.

Vanessa's blood ran cold.

Somebody had broken into the museum.

CHAPTER 18

I'm going to start searching for the afikomen!" Vanessa announced loudly to the seder table. "Sterling, come with me."

"I'm still eating," Sterling protested.

"Nope, you're done now." Vanessa grabbed her brother's arm and tried to wrench him out of his seat.

"Sterling, you should go with your sister," their grandmother advised. "You don't want her to get a head start. The prize this year is pretty good, if I do say so myself."

The afikomen was half a piece of matzah that every year a grown-up (usually their dad, if he was there) hid somewhere around the house during the seder. The kids had to search for it after the meal, and whoever found it got a prize. The tradition was that the seder couldn't be completed without the afikomen, so if it took the kids until midnight to find it, then technically the seder couldn't end until midnight.

It had never taken Vanessa and Sterling *that* long, but sometimes it took half an hour or more. Their dad was impressively good at finding hiding places in a house that he didn't even live in.

"Does anyone else want to try to win this grand prize?" their mom asked. "Jake, Shelley?"

Jake looked horrified. "We'll leave that to the *children*," he said, making it very clear that he was not—and, perhaps, never had been—a child.

But Jake's reluctance was good for Vanessa. Fewer searchers meant it would be more believable if it took a long time to find it. And she needed all the time she could get.

"What's going on?" Sterling asked once she got him out on to the porch. "You think Dad hid it outside? I didn't hear him open the door."

"What's going on is: Someone set off the alarm."

"What?"

"The entry alarm at the museum."

"Yeah, I knew which alarm you're talking about. I just mean . . . How? Who? Are you sure?"

"How: They opened the window covering. Who: I'm going over there to find out. And am I sure: Yes. The alarm sometimes doesn't go off when it should, but it *never* goes off when it shouldn't."

"Maybe it's a raccoon or something," Sterling suggested. "And what do you mean, you're going over there? Now?"

"Yes."

"You can't. We're in the middle of seder."

"I'll be fast."

"You'll be fast!" Sterling threw up his arms in dismay. "What if there *is* an actual intruder there, huh? Then what?"

"Then I'll call 9-1-1."

"And say what? 'Someone broke into this building that I broke into first?' "

"Keep your voice down!" Vanessa hissed. "It's my museum. I have to keep it safe. I'm going."

"Then I'm going with you."

"No, I need you here to buy me time. Look for the afikomen. Look for it until I get back. If they ask where I am, tell them I'm searching outside or in the basement or—"

"No one is ever going to believe that you voluntarily went into the basement," Sterling interrupted.

"Then tell them I'm looking for it in the bathroom! I don't care. Just make it seem like I'm somewhere else in the house. I'll be back as soon as I can. *Then* you can give them the afikomen."

"But if you're not searching for the afikomen, then you can't get the prize."

"I know." Vanessa felt suddenly very mature and responsible as she said, "Sterling, some things are more important than prizes."

And she headed down the steps.

As she ran to the museum in her fancy shoes and dress, she tried to prepare herself for what she might find when she arrived. A thief, come to steal Maria's painting? Was there an art heist in process at this very moment? Or was someone stealing Sterling's baseball cards? Was he right, and would somebody actually want them for something? She would really hate it if Sterling was right. And he would really hate it if his baseball cards got stolen.

She slowed as she crossed the field toward the dark museum. Did she even *want* to know what she would find in there?

Swiftly, silently, like she was nothing more than the breeze itself, Vanessa floated the window curtain open, just a little bit, just enough to see inside.

The museum was silent, dark, and still.

She waited. Nothing moved.

If there was someone in there, they were keeping very well hidden.

"I know you're in there," Vanessa called softly.

No response.

Maybe the museum *hadn't* been broken into. Maybe the alarm just went off by mistake. There was a first time for everything.

Vanessa stepped inside and turned on one of the battery-powered lamps.

Maria's painting was still there, exactly where it was supposed to be. Vanessa breathed a sigh of relief.

Sterling's boring baseball cards were undisturbed, too. As were Honore's watercolors and Rosalie's popsicle stick bridges and Eli's dog toys.

The only sign that an intruder had been there was—

The Bailey Wing.

It was empty.

CHAPTER 19

The next day passed in a daze.

Nobody figured out that Vanessa had gone to the museum rather than search for the afikomen. Sterling had done his job and kept them distracted. Vanessa was bummed to miss out on the prize (a fancy sticker sheet), but that was a sacrifice worth making.

In the afternoon, Vanessa went with the rest of her family to drop her dad off at the airport. He was dressed in military fatigues, and he'd shaved off the scruff of beard that he'd let grow over the past week and a half. He had a full day of traveling ahead of him before arriving in East Africa, where he would start his seven-month deployment.

Their mom pulled up outside of the terminal and popped the trunk. Dad and Sterling got out of the car. Vanessa sat in the back seat and picked at her fingers. She hadn't even bothered to bring her origami paper with her. Why try?

"Vanessa," her mother said, catching her eye in the rearview mirror. "Go say goodbye to your father."

Vanessa sighed and climbed out of the car, slamming the door behind her.

Her dad was hoisting his huge backpack onto his shoulders. "I'm going to miss you both so much," he told them.

"I'm going to miss you, too," Sterling said.

Vanessa grunted.

"Be good," Dad told Sterling. "Help out your mother. I'm counting on you."

Sterling nodded and gave him a big hug. When he pulled away, his forehead was wrinkled, like he was trying not to cry.

"Take care of yourself," Dad said to Vanessa. He opened his arms to her, and she let him embrace her. But she didn't hug him back. *Take care of yourself.* It sounded innocuous, but she knew it wasn't. It was a marching order.

"I love you so much," their dad said. Then he turned and headed off.

"I love you, too!" Sterling called after him.

"I love you," Vanessa echoed, but she made her voice as sarcastic as possible.

Their mom looked at them with concern when they got back in the car. "I know it's hard to say goodbye," she said as they buckled their seatbelts—Sterling taking their dad's place, Vanessa still in the backseat.

"It's not hard," Vanessa said. "It's fine. It couldn't be finer."

She pulled out her phone and texted the rest of the curators: **EMERGENCY MEETING AT THE MUSEUM. ASAP.**

After Vanessa and Sterling, the twins were the first to get to the museum. "I bet I know what this meeting is about," Rosalie said.

"You do?" Vanessa was surprised. How had she already heard about the disappearance of the Bailey artifacts? Had the thief bragged about it?

Rosalie nodded grimly. "I can't believe they're finally tearing down this place after all."

"Wait, *what*?" Vanessa had been sitting atop the admission booth, but now she leapt to her feet. "Where did you hear that?"

"On the sign outside. Hold on, you mean that's *not* what this meeting is about?"

Vanessa climbed back out through the window and saw the brand-new sign that Rosalie was referring to. DEMOLITION SCHEDULED FOR JUNE 1, it said.

This sign was far and away the brightest and cleanest thing anywhere near the museum. It was a wonder that Vanessa hadn't noticed it when she first arrived, but then again, she wasn't really noticing much.

A bitter taste filled her mouth. So the museum was almost over. What did it matter? Her part of the museum was *already* over, taken from her too soon. *All things must come to an end.* That's what her mom had said. They'd always been living on borrowed time. And now their time was up.

Numb, Vanessa went back inside.

"Where are your exhibits, Vanessa?" Honore asked. "You didn't have to clear them out right away. We have until the end of May."

Vanessa opened her mouth to explain, but then Eli came charging in, hollering, "Guess what, guess what, guess what?"

There was no time for them to guess, as he was immediately followed by a German shepherd. But just in case

anyone missed it, he answered his own question: "I got a new dog!"

"Awww!" They all crowded around the animal to pet it. It panted happily and thumped its tail against the floor.

"And check this out," Eli went on. "He's *so* smart. Watch this. Sit!"

The German Shepherd sat.

Eli's eyes sparkled. "Can you believe it? Who'd have thought any dog of mine would be a genius?"

"What's his name?" asked Sterling.

"In honor of Rosalie," Eli replied, "and his extreme intelligence, I've named him . . . Tesla!"

Rosalie flushed with pride.

Tesla leaned heavily, comfortingly against Vanessa's legs. She patted his head tentatively. He was a little big and slobbery, but he wasn't that bad. "How could you get a new dog? Don't you still miss Einstein?" she asked.

"Of *course* I still miss Einstein. Einstein was the best." Eli bent down and let Tesla lick his face. "Tesla is the best, too," he added.

"That's not how 'best' works," said Honore.

"It is now." Eli shrugged. "I'm going to take some stuff from the Einstein Wing home today, so Tesla can use it. Not all of it. Some of it is too much Einstein to ever belong

to another dog. But, like, the water bowl. Tesla can use his water bowl." Tesla had already started sniffing at one of Einstein's old toys, so Eli said, "I'll take that home for him, too."

Then his eye caught the empty Bailey Wing. "Hey, Vanessa, did you take your stuff home, too? Why—did you get a new best friend to use it?"

He laughed until he saw the look on Vanessa's face, then stopped abruptly.

"We were robbed," Vanessa said.

Everyone gasped in shock—except Sterling, who had gotten the basic facts last night.

"What? Why? Who did this?" Vanessa's friends had a million questions.

"How did they sneak past my security system?" Rosalie demanded.

"They didn't. Your system worked perfectly. I just didn't get here fast enough to catch them."

"This is a *heist*," Eli said, his eyes wide. "And actual heist! Like at the Isabella Stewart Gardner Museum. That museum offered a reward, right? We should do that!"

"They offered a ten million dollar reward," Vanessa said, "which is a little outside of our budget. Also, it didn't work, remember? They never got the paintings back."

"Oh, yeah." Eli's shoulders sagged.

"What *I* don't get," Honore said, "is why they only took Vanessa's stuff. I mean, my watercolors are *very* pretty. You'd think the thief would want to steal at least one of them."

"Honore, it's not, like, an *insult* to not be the victim of a robbery," Rosalie told her.

"And why not take Sterling's baseball cards?" Eli wondered. "Those are worth a lot. Or at least he keeps claiming they are. Plus Maria's painting! I mean, talk about pretty!"

"I bet Maria's painting would be too heavy for most thieves," Rosalie mused.

"Still, why Vanessa's collection? It's all basically—no offense—worthless."

Vanessa wasn't offended. She knew it was. Used clothes and pieces of paper and frayed friendship bracelets—it was worthless to the world, and priceless to Vanessa.

Sterling groaned and sat down on the floor next to Tesla. "Isn't it obvious what happened? Bailey came and took all her stuff."

Vanessa buried her face in Tesla's fur.

"But . . ." Honore said. "Why? And how?"

"I'm going to guess it's because she's the worst, as usual," Eli said.

"And because the exhibition made her look bad," Vanessa said. "It told the truth about her, and all the horrible stuff she's done."

"The exhibition didn't make her look *that* bad," Rosalie said.

"Well, then, maybe she just didn't want me to have it. Because she knew it made me happy, and she wanted to make sure I couldn't be happy without her. Who knows? All that matters is that she stole it."

The artifacts had been the proof. Proof that Bailey and Vanessa really had been best friends. Proof that they'd shared jokes and secrets and crushes and a life, a whole life, built out of place mats and friendship bracelets, pottery and books and hand-me-down headbands and joint-custody dolls. These little things were the only proof Vanessa had, and now even they were gone, leaving Vanessa with nothing.

"So what are you going to *do*?" Eli asked.

Vanessa gave Tesla one last long hug. Then she stood up, clenched her fists, and said, "I'm going to confront her."

CHAPTER 20

After school on Wednesdays, Bailey usually hung out at her family's restaurant, so that was where Vanessa went to track her down. There was no guarantee that Bailey would be there—she might be over at Lisa's or one of her other new friends' houses; she might be at home; she might have stayed late at school. She didn't have gymnastics practice on Wednesdays, or at least she hadn't, last time Vanessa knew her whole schedule by heart. The restaurant was Vanessa's best shot.

And she got lucky. She opened the door to Pancho's and there was Bailey, sitting on a barstool, doing her homework.

"Table for one?" asked the host at the front of the restaurant. He was new. Anyone who worked at Pancho's for any length of time knew that when Vanessa showed up, it was for Bailey, not for food.

"No, thank you," Vanessa said.

Bailey looked up at the sound of her voice. She set down her pencil. Vanessa tried to read the expression on her face. Was she guilty? Angry? Searching for an escape route?

Vanessa marched up to the bar and sat down next to her ex–best friend.

"You're so lucky not to have Mrs. Petrie for math," Bailey greeted her. "She never explains *anything*, and then she gives us these worksheets like we're supposed to know—"

"Give me my stuff back," Vanessa interrupted.

There was a long pause. Bailey's eyes shifted from side to side. "What stuff?" she asked at last.

"The stuff you stole from my museum."

"I have no clue what you're talking about."

Vanessa slapped her hands down on the table. "I know you took it, Bailey. You didn't even try to cover your tracks. You left behind everything else and took only the pieces that were about you. Nobody but you would have any reason to steal our old Halloween costumes and games and

pictures. You even did it during the Passover seder, when you knew I wouldn't be there to stop you."

"No, I didn't," Bailey said.

"And why should I believe you?" Vanessa's hands were shaking. "You're a liar. You lie all the time. You said we'd be best friends forever. That was a *lie*, Bailey. And now you're lying about stealing from me. I can't trust you. Not with anything."

When Bailey responded, she didn't sound contrite. She sounded furious. "How dare you," she said, "show up at my family's restaurant and accuse me of lying and stealing? I get that you're mad at me, but that doesn't give you any excuse to start making up rumors about me."

"It's not a rumor if it's true," Vanessa said, which she noted fleetingly was the same argument she'd made before they released the first issue of *Shh!* "Look, just give me back my stuff and you'll never have to talk to me again."

"I can't," Bailey said.

Vanessa's face felt hot, like she was breathing fire. "It's sad, really," she spat out. "All this time, I wanted you to come to the museum so you could see how good our friendship was. I honestly believed that if you saw it all laid out, in order, with labels, with everything *so clear*, you would finally get it.

"But it turns out the joke's on me. You came, and you saw it, and then you just had to destroy it all."

And with that, Vanessa turned and left.

Outside, in the parking lot, Vanessa took several deep breaths. She thought Bailey might come running out after her, to admit or apologize, or even just to continue the argument. But she didn't.

Vanessa paced the parking lot, past the bike shop where she wouldn't let her dad take them, past the pizza parlor and the art supply store and the FedEx and the photo printing place that Vanessa's mom said was probably a front for something illegal because how could anyone stay in business just printing photos in this day and age? It wasn't a particularly fun shopping plaza, but it was where Vanessa had spent so much of her life, because it was where Bailey was.

HONK!

Vanessa realized she'd been walking down the middle of the pavement. She jumped out of the way, on to a grassy strip, so a car could pass.

And then something caught her eye. Something she had never noticed before.

It was on the small grassy strip between two rows of parked cars. It was a marble block, about as tall as Vanessa, with a small marble trough surrounding it.

Vanessa was gripped with a sense of déjà vu. That sculpture—it looked like the sculpture in Maria's painting.

"You are overreacting, kid," Vanessa whispered to herself.

Still, she stepped closer. She walked around to the opposite side of the statue. And on it, between a parked Honda and a Subaru hatchback, she saw the angelic face with the hole in the middle of its lips.

Just like in the painting.

Unlike in Maria's version, there was no water pouring out of this angel's mouth. The trough was bone-dry. But otherwise, it was the same.

Vanessa's heart was racing. Were angelic marble fountain things common decorations? Or was it possible that *this* was the very same sculpture that Maria had painted? But how had it gotten from that beautiful field in the picture to the middle of this shopping center? Why had she, Vanessa, never noticed it before?

Could it be that she'd spent all this time wishing to go to the beautiful place in the painting, and all along she *had* been there, had been going there for *years*, and simply hadn't recognized it?

There was a little bronze plaque on the base of the trough. Vanessa crouched down to brush away the overgrown grass that obscured it, and she read:

THE ANGEL OPENS HIS MOUTH AND SPEAKS THE TRUTH

She pulled out her phone and typed in that exact phrase, plus "Maria," plus "painting."

And she got a hit.

CHAPTER 21

The Angel Opens His Mouth and Speaks the Truth is one of the earliest of Mariko Marsden's known paintings. She is believed to have painted it during the summer of 1970, which she spent in a small town on the outskirts of Cleveland, Ohio.

Because this is such an early work and, at the time, Marsden was unknown in the art world (in fact, she was still going by her birth name of Maria Madden!), there exists no visual or written description of the painting. For all intents and purposes, the work is lost.

Were it not for a brief mention of the painting in a letter that she wrote to her mother that summer, we would not even know of its existence. There remains debate as to whether it is in fact its own painting, or whether this was just an early working title for Marsden's *The Number One Song in Heaven.*

Vanessa was back at home, in her room, picking at her skin as she pieced together what she had learned and what she suspected.

Have you heard of Mariko Marsden? she texted the rest of the curators. The responses came instantly.

Rosalie

Of course.

Honore

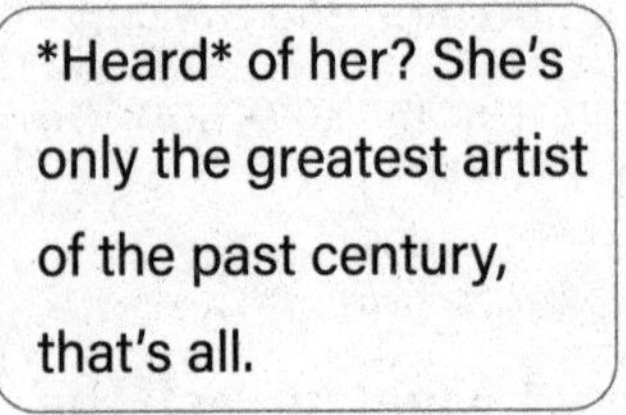

Sterling

We saw one of her paintings at the Museum of Modern Art, remember?

Eli

Is she from Mars?! Get it, MARSden? lol jk. Yeah I've heard of her.

Mariko Marsden, one of the world's most famous living artists. Here is what Vanessa had learned about her in the past couple hours:

She was now in her seventies and living on Bainbridge Island, outside of Seattle. (Vanessa had just looked this up.)

She was half Finnish (on her dad's side of the family) and half Japanese (on her mom's side).

More than fifty years ago, she had spent a summer in a small town near Cleveland—a town that sounded a lot like Edgewood Falls.

Back then, she had gone by the name Maria—just like the artist who painted the piece in the museum.

And she had made a painting that no one had seen, and named it after a statue in the parking lot of Bailey's family's restaurant's shopping plaza.

Vanessa messaged the group again. **I think she's Maria. I think she made our painting.**

Again, the responses came fast and furious.

Rosalie

No way!! How do you know?

Honore

omg omg I can't believe that MY ARTWORK is in a museum right next to MARIKO MARSDEN'S ARTWORK!

Sterling

If that's *actually* a Mairko Marsden—which I doubt—it'd be worth like a million bucks.

Eli just responded with a string of emojis.

Vanessa set down her phone and tried to figure out what to do. If this really *was* a painting by the famed Mariko Marsden—and Vanessa believed that it was; who cared what Sterling thought—they couldn't just leave it

there while the museum got demolished. But where else could it go? If Vanessa showed up at home with a six-foot-wide oil painting, her mother was not going to believe that she just happened to find it on the street.

She needed to ask Mariko Marsden if this really was her painting, and, if it was, what she wanted to do with it. But that turned out to be not so easy. While there were plenty of fan accounts with convincing-sounding names like "TheRealMarikoMarsden," further digging showed that none of them actually belonged to the artist herself. If she had a website or email address of her own, Vanessa couldn't find it. One website promised "complete contact info for every celeb, including *Mariko Marsden*!" but it charged $49.99 for every search and seemed deeply sketchy.

"Vanessa!" her mom called from downstairs. "Will you set the table?"

"I'm doing research!" Vanessa yelled back.

The problem, Vanessa felt, was that Mariko Marsden was *old*. Obviously there were plenty of old people who were very comfortable on the internet, like Vanessa's grandmother, who was always trying to convince her to join various social networks so they could be "friends." But a lot of members of that generation *could* live without the internet, and so they *did* live without the internet.

This made Vanessa think: Did anybody who *wasn't* old know how to get in touch with Mariko Marsden?

She sleuthed further and googled "Mariko Marsden + children."

No luck. The artist had never had any kids.

"Mariko Marsden + family," she tried next. This turned up an article with the first names of Mariko's brothers, Basil and Dax. Vanessa tried searching for "Basil Marsden" and "Dax Marsden" to no avail, before remembering that they probably hadn't taken on Mariko's made-up last name.

"Vanessa!" her mother shouted again. "Dinner!"

"I'm not hungry!" Vanessa yelled.

She tried "Dax Madden" and found a few mentions of him online. He'd written a letter to the editor of a local newspaper in New Mexico. He'd reviewed a lawn maintenance provider. And there was a photo of him from ten years ago, with two women identified as his wife and daughter, and a toddler. His granddaughter, Georgie.

Jackpot.

Vanessa searched for "Georgie Madden" and found social media accounts for eight people. The first looked to be in her fifties. The second was a man. The third was Norwegian.

But the fourth Georgie Madden she looked up was thirteen years old and lived in Taos, New Mexico.

"Yes!" Vanessa pumped her fist.

"Vanessa." She looked up to see her mother standing in the door. "Sterling and I are already done eating."

"I told you, I'm not hungry," Vanessa said.

Her mom sighed and returned downstairs.

And Vanessa sent a message to Georgie Madden:

Hi Georgie,

You don't know me, but my name is Vanessa, and I live in Ohio. This is all going to sound super random, but here goes:

I'm pretty sure that you're Mariko Marsden's grandniece. And I'm also pretty sure that I've found a painting that your great-aunt did more than fifty years ago. I know this is weird, but can you ask her if this is *The Angel Opens His Mouth and Speaks the Truth*? And, if it is, can you ask her what she wants to do with it?

Thank you.

Sincerely,

Vanessa, age 11

Vanessa attached a photo of Maria's painting. And then she waited.

After five minutes of no response, and not even a read receipt, Vanessa was surprised to realize that she was starving. "There was really no way to see that coming," she said, and she went downstairs to see if there was any dinner left.

CHAPTER 22

Days passed, but no matter how many times Vanessa checked her inbox, she had no response from Georgie Madden. Maybe Georgie didn't read messages from strangers. Maybe she wasn't actually Mariko Marsden's grandniece. Maybe she just thought Vanessa was creepy for tracking her down.

Meanwhile, visitors kept coming to the museum. They didn't mind that the Bailey Wing was gone, not when there was so much else for them to see. But they did mind that the building was going to be torn down in just over a month. Everyone wanted to know *why.*

"Because nothing gold can stay," Vanessa answered. This was a line from a Robert Frost poem they'd read at school. She didn't really know what it meant at the time. Now she did.

One afternoon, it was just Vanessa and Rosalie at the museum, collecting admission and answering guests' questions. "Where's Honore?" Vanessa asked.

"I don't know," Rosalie replied, wrestling with the battery cover on one of their lanterns.

"Really?" Vanessa asked.

"Where's Sterling?" Rosalie asked back.

Vanessa shrugged. "No clue."

"If you don't know where your brother is," Rosalie said, "then why should I know where my sister is?"

"Because you two are *identical twins*," Vanessa reminded her. "And best friends." Back when Vanessa and Bailey were best friends, Vanessa always knew where Bailey was, in those rare times when they weren't together.

"That doesn't mean we have to do everything together," Rosalie said.

"But you *could* do everything together," Vanessa pointed out.

"Yeah, but we don't want to. Yes!" Rosalie fist pumped as she finally managed to pry open the lantern's battery compartment.

"I guess that makes sense," Vanessa said dubiously. It seemed like such a good thing, to have a built-in best friend. But the better she got to know Rosalie and Honore, the more different they seemed. And maybe Rosalie also found her sister annoying sometimes. "I don't want to do everything with my brother, either. I didn't even want him to be part of the museum."

"I've actually always wondered about that." Rosalie popped in four new triple-A batteries and looked at Vanessa. "Why *does* Sterling hang out here?"

"To annoy me?" Vanessa suggested, but she knew that wasn't it. The truth was, she had never given *any* thought to why her brother wanted to be part of the museum. She straightened a pile of photocopied museum maps as she pondered Rosalie's question. "I assume he's here because the museum is awesome. Right? Isn't that why we're all here?"

"It's definitely awesome," Rosalie agreed. "But, I don't know, he's in high school. Shouldn't he be hanging out with other high schoolers?"

"He hangs out with friends his age, too." But as Vanessa said this, she realized that might not be true. She tried to think of the last time her brother had invited

somebody over, or gone to a friend's house, or the movies, or a sleepover, or anything. Nothing came to mind. "Do you think it's weird?" she asked.

Rosalie shrugged. "My brother's a year older than yours, and he wouldn't be caught dead playing with Honore and me. Maybe Sterling is just nicer than Konnor."

Vanessa picked at a bug bite on her arm as she considered this. Just like Maria's painting, Sterling's presence at the museum was a mystery. One that hadn't even occurred to Vanessa to try to solve it until now.

"When the museum gets knocked down, I bet he's going to be as sad as we are," Rosalie said.

But Vanessa was sad *now.* She didn't need the physical building to disappear to start mourning it. After all, her collection was already gone. "The museum is already pretty much over," she said.

"The museum is nowhere near over," Rosalie said. "Look around. We've had more visitors this week than ever before."

This was true. As word spread that the museum would close on June first, more and more people wanted to see it before it was too late.

"But *I* don't have anything for them to look at," Vanessa reminded Rosalie. She walked over to the now-empty

Bailey Wing and gestured around. None of the museum guests came to this area. There was nothing for them to look at.

"So put up another display," Rosalie said.

"I can't. My entire Bailey collection was here. I don't have anything left."

Rosalie dusted off one of the empty display cases where Vanessa's exhibition had been. "I meant, put up a *new* display. About something else. Not Bailey."

"I don't . . ." Vanessa stared at Rosalie. "I don't have anything else. I'm not really good at science, like you, or art, like Honore. I don't collect baseball cards—or anything, really."

"You could start collecting something," Rosalie suggested.

"Like what?"

"Anything you want." Rosalie shrugged. "Or you could do an exhibition of all that stuff."

She pointed at Vanessa's hands, and Vanessa looked down at the paper crane she was folding. "My origami?" she asked.

"Yes! Why not?"

Vanessa felt a smile growing across her face. She *could* put up an exhibition of her paper crafts. They didn't serve any purpose outside of the time when she was making them, when they kept her fingers busy. After she was done making something, it just took up space. Why not put it on display, where other people could enjoy it? She could organize the collection by species of animal. Or maybe she could write a label about the history of paper-folding crafts. Maybe she could even work with Rosalie, and have Rosalie provide science facts about the animals and she could model them with paper. It would be fun to have a project just the two of them.

Then she shook her head. "The museum is still getting knocked down in a few weeks," she reminded Rosalie.

"I know." Rosalie ran fingers down her face like tears.

"So there's no point to putting up an origami exhibition," Vanessa said, "when it's just going to get taken down again."

"Maybe," Rosalie said. "But it would be good for as long as it lasts. Isn't that reason enough to do it?"

Vanessa was silent for a long moment, digesting this.

"That's, like, really wise," she said at last.

"I mean, I did get a hundred on my last lab report, so yeah," Rosalie said. "I'm pretty smart."

Impulsively, Vanessa threw her arms around Rosalie.

Rosalie giggled and hugged her back. "We should

hang out more," she said. "*Without* your brother and my sister."

"Yeah." Vanessa nodded slowly. She hadn't even known that was an option. "I guess we should."

Back at home, Vanessa gathered up her origami from throughout the house and laid it all out in her bedroom. She started sorting through it. Some of the pieces just weren't very good—you couldn't even tell what they were supposed to be—so she put those in a pile to stay home. She went through a list of origami creatures and highlighted all the ones she hadn't tried yet. She read a couple articles about the history of origami and made notes on the smallest paper crane in history (which was supposedly only one millimeter) and the largest (which had a wingspan of nearly 270 feet—she saw a photo of it in the middle of a football field).

Sterling popped his head into her bedroom. "Hey, have you heard from Dad today?"

"No. And I don't want to." Since he'd left, their dad had sent Vanessa the same number of texts and phone

calls that he usually did when he was on deployment. But she'd mostly ignored them. "Hey," she added, thinking about Rosalie's remarks earlier, "why are you always at the museum?"

"*You're* always at the museum," he pointed out.

"Yeah, I know, but you usually don't want to do the stuff that I do."

"That's because most of the stuff that you do is dumb."

"Rosalie thinks it's weird that you're there and not hanging out with people your own age."

Sterling's face turned so red that it was almost purple. "Rosalie can mind her own freakin' business," he snapped. He stomped out of the room, yelling behind him, "Just tell me if you hear from Dad."

Vanessa went back to organizing and planning for her new exhibition.

After a few minutes, she set down her origami. She felt guilty about upsetting Sterling. She hadn't been trying to *actually* make him feel bad. She'd just been curious, and, okay, teasing him a little. But it seemed like she'd gone too far. There were some buttons you just didn't press. Like how Sterling would happily make fun of her for her fear of spiders, but he never said anything about her picking habit. They both knew that you didn't touch the really shameful stuff.

Vanessa climbed through her piles of origami and headed down the hall to Sterling's room, so she could say something nice and smooth things over, or at least give him the chance to make fun of her in return and even the score. When she opened his door, he jerked around from his computer, minimizing the window on his screen as fast as possible. But not fast enough.

"What did that say?" Vanessa asked.

"Nothing."

"Was that today's news?"

"No."

Vanessa marched over and reopened the window that Sterling had been looking at. He didn't try to stop her.

TWO DEAD AND SIXTEEN MISSING AS MISSILE STRIKE HITS U.S. MILITARY BASE IN SUDAN read the headline.

Vanessa and her brother stared at each other. "Is Dad in Sudan?" she whispered.

"I don't know. He just said East Africa."

"Is Sudan in East Africa?"

Sterling googled it. It was.

"There are a lot of places in East Africa," Sterling said, his voice unsteady. "It's huge. Dad could be anywhere."

"Right," Vanessa agreed, sitting down on Sterling's bed. "But what if he's in Sudan?"

"Even then, he probably isn't one of the people who di—" He swallowed the end of the word. "Who are in this article. I mean, what are the odds that it's *our* dad?"

"It's *somebody's* dad," Vanessa answered.

She and Sterling looked at each other silently.

"Have you tried calling him?" Vanessa asked. Her brother nodded. "I'm going to try again," she said.

She dialed and waited. The phone rang once, twice. After five rings, she heard her father's voice. "This is Edgar Lepp, leave a message." *Beep.*

Vanessa hung up. "Let's ask Mom."

They headed downstairs, where their mother was watching her TV channel. "In St. Louis, a man trying to install an in-ground swimming pool in his backyard encountered an unusual surprise," the female anchor said. "Three dozen bowling balls just underneath the surface! Duncan Ross discovered that the previous owners had buried balls from the local bowling alley to help with drainage. Can you believe it?"

"Mom," Vanessa began.

"Shh, I wrote this segment," their mom said, not looking away from the TV.

"Let this be a lesson: Look out for unexpected bowling balls!" said the male anchor.

"Good lesson, right?" their mom said.

Vanessa and Sterling stood in front of the screen. "Is Dad okay?" Sterling asked.

"I assume so . . ." Their mother's voice trailed off as Sterling held up the article about the attack on his phone. "Oh."

She took the phone and put on her glasses so she could scroll through it. The corners of her mouth pulled together tighter and tighter. "You tried calling him?" she asked.

They both nodded.

"I'm going to try again," she said.

She got the same voicemail greeting that Vanessa had.

"I'm texting him, too," their mom said. "And emailing. You never know." Her fingers flew over her tablet.

"Is he okay?" Vanessa asked in a small voice.

"Come here." Their mom opened her arms to them and they both crawled onto either side of the couch. "I think he's safe," she said. "I honestly do."

"How do you know?" Vanessa asked.

"I don't know. That's just what my gut tells me. This has happened before, you know, and he's always been fine."

It was true—it seemed like every time her dad deployed, there would be a couple days when they didn't hear from him at all. If a soldier was killed, there would be an official communications blackout, so nobody on base could reach anyone off base until the general in charge said it was

okay. Sometimes the base's Wi-Fi would get knocked out, or sometimes he'd have to go out into the field for forty-eight hours or he'd be dealing with some other work crisis and so he couldn't be in touch. These things happened, but he always came back.

But maybe sometime he wouldn't come back. And maybe this was that time.

"What if he never comes home?" Vanessa's voice broke.

"That would be terrible," her mom replied. "It would be unspeakably tragic. It would be one of the worst things that could possibly happen. And we would find a way through it. But I don't want you to get caught up in 'what-ifs.' As far as we know, that's *not* what's happened. As far as we know, he's fine. Imagining that he's not won't help anything. If we ever find out that he's not fine, we'll deal with it then."

Vanessa knew that her mom was being rational and making sense. It didn't matter. She could hardly even hear her mother's words over the thoughts in her brain.

What if I never see my father again?

What if the last time I ever saw him, I yelled at him and didn't even want to say that I loved him?

What if he's gone forever and I never even stopped picking for him?

What if he died thinking that I'm a bad daughter?

Vanessa tucked her body into a tight little ball and, with her face pressed against her mother's lap, she sobbed.

"Oh, honey." Her mom stroked her back. "It's okay. He'll be okay. We'll hear from him soon. I know we will."

"What if we don't?"

"Your father knew what he was getting into when he joined the armed forces," her mother said. "He has always known and accepted that he might someday have to sacrifice himself to defend us all. It's highly unlikely, but it's a possibility that he made peace with long ago. And if that's ever what happens, he will do it with grace and dignity and his eyes wide open."

"Why?" Vanessa choked out. "Why would he choose a job that meant leaving us?"

Her mother ran her hand through Vanessa's hair, gently working through the tangles. "He chose a job doing what he thinks is right and important and fulfilling. Leaving us wasn't the point. It's just a terrible, unavoidable side effect."

"Dad's smart." That was Sterling's voice. "He's strong and brave and clever. He can take care of himself."

But Vanessa knew that this was just her big brother trying to make her feel better. Bad things happened all the time. It didn't matter how smart and strong and brave and clever you were. The bad things came anyway.

CHAPTER 23

"Did you start planning the origami exhibition?" Rosalie asked as they took their seats in homeroom the next day.

Vanessa blinked at her. Her excitement about displaying her origami in the museum felt like it came from a different lifetime. "Sort of," she said. She set her phone on her desk, where she could see it.

"Um, Vanessa?" Rosalie pointed at the phone. Mr. Howard was a real stickler about them. If he saw students even glancing at their phones for a second in his class, he would take them away.

"I have a note from my mom," Vanessa said.

They had argued that morning over whether or not

Vanessa should have to go to school. "What if we get news about Dad and I'm at school?" Vanessa had said.

"Then I'll come get you," her mom had said. "It will be good for you to keep to your normal schedule, be around your friends. Sitting at home all day and worrying isn't going to help anything."

Overnight, her mom had reached out to the other military wives she'd stayed in touch with, asking if they'd heard anything. They'd all seen the news story, but nobody knew anything more than that. Which meant that the communication blackout was still in place.

"What if Dad calls me and I miss it because I'm not allowed to use my phone at school?" Vanessa had countered. And so her mom wrote a note to her teachers saying that, due to "extenuating family circumstances," Vanessa was allowed to look at her phone whenever she needed to. That was the compromise.

But Vanesa's phone stayed stubbornly dark. No calls from her dad. No messages from Georgie Madden. She refreshed her inbox just in case. Nothing.

"Is everything okay?" Rosalie asked.

"We haven't heard from my dad in a little while," Vanessa said. When Rosalie's eyes widened, she hastened to add, "It's probably fine. I think I'm overreacting."

"Where's your dad?" Bailey asked.

Vanessa looked over at her. She hadn't even realized that Bailey had been listening. "East Africa," she replied. "There was an attack there yesterday. A couple American soldiers were killed, but they haven't released their names yet."

Rosalie covered her mouth with her hands.

"I'm so sorry," Bailey said.

"Like I said, he's probably fine."

"I know," Bailey agreed, "but it's still really scary and horrible to think that he might not be."

Vanessa felt a surge of calm—Bailey understood, Bailey always understood, Bailey knew Vanessa better than anyone—followed by a surge of sadness—she had missed this so much, the comfort of having Bailey on her side, and if her dad's absence meant that Bailey would come back, then maybe that was a fair trade—followed by a surge of anger. It was too many conflicting emotions. The anger was what she went with.

"Since when do you care?" Vanessa said to Bailey. "Everything I love eventually goes away. That's just what happens. You're the one who taught me that."

At that moment, Mr. Howard called everyone to attention. So if Bailey had any response, she kept it to herself.

After school, Vanessa got home before her mother or brother. She watched her phone (nothing happened) and watched the news on TV (lots of stuff happened, but all of it was depressing and none of it was updates on the attack in Sudan).

Her phone buzzed and her heart rose into her throat—but it was just Eli saying that he was at the museum, and was she coming today? She ignored it.

She went into the kitchen to get a glass of water, and then she saw something out the window so terrifying that her heart stopped beating.

It was two soldiers, walking down her street, in uniform.

Vanessa felt dizzy. The glass slipped from her hand and smashed into pieces on the floor. She made no move to clean it up. She was frozen in place.

Every military family knew that this was how they told you, if your parent or child or spouse died while on duty. Uniformed officers would come to your door. They would sit you down. They would give you the news. That's how it worked. They were the grim reapers of the military.

If these two officers were here to knock on her door, Vanessa wasn't going to let them. Her dad would stay alive

until anyone told her otherwise—and *no one* was going to tell her otherwise.

She bolted upstairs and closed herself in her bedroom. There was no lock on her door, so she did the next-best thing: sticking her desk chair in front of it, and then piling books onto the chair to make it too heavy to move. Then she put on some music, and turned it up as loud as it would go. Her bedroom faced the back of the house. If those two service members knocked on her door, she would not see them. She would not hear them. They could not exist.

Vanessa paced her room in tight circles. She picked at a patch of dry skin on her elbow. She texted her dad again. She needed to do something.

She wrote another message:

Georgie, it's me again, Vanessa. Sorry to keep messaging you. You probably think I'm crazy, but I really need your help.

I found an abandoned museum, and I fixed it up. I made it work again. I found what I'm 96% sure is your great-aunt's painting in there. It was all alone, forgotten. I put it back on display.

But a lot of bad stuff has happened. My best friend stopped being my best friend. My dad is in the army and I

haven't heard from him recently and I'm trying not to over-react but I think he might be dead. The museum with your great-aunt's painting is getting torn down. Things used to be good, but they're bad now.

I know none of this has anything to do with you, and you don't have any reason to care about it at all. But I need to fix something. I need to return this artwork to the person it belongs to.

The painting shows two girls having a picnic together and on the back it says "For Richelle." So I think one of the girls is your great-aunt, and the other is Richelle, and your great-aunt painted this and gave it to Richelle. And so it should go back to Richelle or to your great-aunt. It shouldn't just be abandoned here.

Their friendship mattered. The painting is beautiful. Someone should treasure it. This isn't the way it should end.

I just need your help.

Sincerely,
Vanessa, age 11

P.S. Sorry again to be weird and random.

P.P.S. Please write back soon.

"Vanessa?" She heard her mom's voice dimly, almost drowned out by the music. She saw her door handle turn, and then the door got stuck against her chair. "Honey, are you in there? I saw a broken glass in the kitchen—you really need to clean that up or someone could cut themselves. Will you turn down that music, please?"

Vanessa stopped the track. The quiet surprised her.

"Can I come in?" her mom asked.

"Yeah. Just give me a minute." Vanessa moved aside piles of books until finally the chair was light enough to scooch out of the way. She opened the door.

Her mother took in all the books strewn around the room. "What's going on?" she asked.

"There were . . ." If she didn't say it, maybe it wouldn't be real. "There were two officers in uniform on our street."

"Oh, honey." Her mother sat down on her bed.

"I thought they were coming to talk to us. That's Occam's Razor."

"I can see why you thought that," her mother said.

"But . . . they weren't?" Vanessa asked. A flicker of hope lodged itself in her chest.

"They weren't," her mom confirmed. "Nobody called me. Nobody came to my office. They were just walking down the street. They weren't here for us."

"Oh," Vanessa said. She let out a long exhale. The worst hadn't come. Not yet. There was still a chance for anything to happen. Maybe something bad. But maybe something good.

"Come here," Vanessa's mom said, and Vanessa climbed onto the bed next to her and leaned against her. "I'm sorry you were scared," her mom said.

"And I'm sorry I broke the glass," Vanessa said.

Her mom kissed the top of her head. "It's completely okay. It was an accident. But you do still have to clean it up."

"Yeah, I know. Will you get the broom out of the basement for me?"

Her mother smiled at her and squeezed her shoulders. "You can do hard things, Vanessa. You can get the broom yourself."

CHAPTER 24

The next day, there was still no word from Vanessa's father. This wasn't the longest they'd ever gone without hearing from him. But it was getting close.

If he'd been killed, the army would have told them by now. Right?

But if he was alive, then how come he hadn't been in touch?

To take her mind off things, Vanessa packed up her origami and took it to the museum. But when she got there, her heart sank. There was a woman standing in the cul-de-sac, staring up at the museum. She was tall and skinny, with short-cropped gray hair, leather boots, and a brightly patterned shawl.

She was probably there to work on the plans to demolish it. Even if she wasn't, even if she was just some random adult taking an interest in an abandoned building, Vanessa couldn't go in there while she was watching.

Ugh.

Vanessa stopped walking purposefully toward the museum and instead pretended like she'd come to this park to search for four-leaf clovers. "Oh, shucks, only three-leaf clovers here," Vanessa said, trying to make it seem believable. "Guess I'll just go home."

Then the woman was in front of her. "Are you Vanessa?" she asked.

Vanessa jolted back.

"I'm Mariko Marsden," the woman said. "But you might know me as Maria."

Vanessa stared at her in stunned silence.

Mariko Marsden stared back.

"How . . ." Vanessa began. She cleared her throat. "It is such an honor to meet you. Wow. You're, like, *really* famous. Sorry. That was weird. What are you doing here?"

"My grand-niece Georgie shared your message with me," Mariko Marsden explained. "She told me it was important. When you said you had found *The Angel Opens His Mouth and Speaks the Truth* in a small town in Ohio,

I assumed it was Edgewood Falls, since that's where I painted it and where I left it. So I got here and asked where I might find an abandoned museum. The librarian directed me here."

"You . . . what?" Vanessa's mind was blown. "You came all the way here based on *that*? You could've just emailed."

Mariko Marsden shrugged. "I don't believe in email."

Vanessa stood stock still. She couldn't figure out what was more astonishing: that she was meeting one of the most famous artists in the world, that she was meeting Maria, or that she had successfully solved the mystery of the painting. None of it seemed possible.

"Well, I'm going to see the painting," Mariko Marsden announced, and she began striding toward the museum.

Vanessa found her voice. "Of course! You should see the painting. I mean, you came all this way. And it's your painting in the first place. So it's not like you need my permission or anything . . ." She ran ahead of the artist and swept aside the garbage bag at the window. "You're the first grown-up to be here," Vanessa told her. "We actually have a 'no adults' rule."

Mariko Marsden raised a single eyebrow. She didn't have any hair over her eyes—instead, she'd drawn on lines

where her eyebrows should have been. There was something else odd about her eyes, too, but Vanessa wasn't immediately sure what it was.

"We can make an exception to the no-adults rule for you," Vanessa hastened to assure her.

"Thank you," Mariko Marsden said dryly, and then Vanessa realized what it was. Mariko Marsden didn't have eyelashes, either.

"I just want to warn you," Vanessa said, "you're probably used to really fancy and professional museums. This is . . . not that."

"I am setting my expectations accordingly." Mariko Marsden crawled through the window with surprising ease for someone her age. Vanessa scrambled through after her.

Inside, the artist took a long look around the room, taking in all the signs and collections. Vanessa wondered what she was thinking, tried to see it for the first time through her eyes.

"Here's a map." Vanessa handed it to her, just like she would for any visitor. "Let me know if you have any questions about the exhibits." She decided against charging Mariko Marsden an admission fee.

Mariko Marsden saw the large oil painting from across the room, and her face lit up. She strode straight over to it, with Vanessa one step behind.

"There it is," she murmured. "How marvelous."

Vanessa and the artist stood side-by-side, taking it in.

"I haven't seen this painting in fifty years," Mariko Marsden said. "I didn't think I would ever see it again. Just look at it!" She seemed as unable to believe this turn of events as Vanessa was. She reached out a hand and stroked the canvas.

Vanessa made a little choking noise, because the very first thing she'd learned about museums was that you were *not* allowed to touch the art. Not unless it was like Rosalie's science projects, which specifically had labels saying "please touch."

Though she supposed the rules were different if it was *your* artwork. After all, Honore could touch her watercolors as much as she wanted. It was just hard to suddenly start thinking of the painting, which had for so long felt like Vanessa's, as though it now belonged to this stranger.

Mariko Marsden's fingers skated across her hairless eyebrows, then pulled a little plastic band out of her pocket. She twisted it around her thumb without ever taking her

eyes off the artwork. "How on earth did you find this? How did you find *me*?"

So Vanessa explained how she had discovered the museum, and then discovered this painting in the side room. How she had been searching online for "Maria" without any success, and then found the statue in the parking lot and pieced it all together. She steeled herself for this grown-up artist to say something grown-up-like about how abandoned museums were dangerous places, but Mariko Marsden didn't even seem to notice that part.

"I'm glad the statue is still there," she said instead. "It used to be our meeting point, Richelle's and mine. I should go see that while I'm in town, too."

"It doesn't look like it does in your painting anymore," Vanessa warned her. "They built up a shopping center around it."

"Of course they did." Mariko Marsden shook her head. "That's the way of the world, isn't it: pave paradise and put up a parking lot. *This* is why preservation is so important! If we don't work to protect beauty, it will disappear in favor of whatever people *think* they want at that exact moment in time. Beauty is hard to find, harder still to create, and easy to destroy. Yet it is human nature to destroy and start

anew." The plastic band twirled faster in Mariko Marsden's fingers. "Which reminds me, is this building really getting demolished? What a shame!"

Vanessa nodded. "We—my friends and I—we've turned it into a really good museum. I think it is, anyway. We all curated our own exhibitions. I was just about to install a new one about origami. That section is for my brother's baseball cards. That's the Science Wing over there. That's the Einstein Wing."

"The Einstein Wing isn't part of the Science Wing?" asked Mariko.

"It's an exhibit about a dog named Einstein."

"I see. Not a particularly bright dog, I gather?"

"How did you know?"

Mariko raised her painted eyebrows again. "I have a great appreciation for irony."

"We have other ideas for collections, too. But once the museum is gone . . . well, it doesn't really matter anymore."

"I suppose it doesn't," Mariko said.

"So that's why your painting can't stay here," Vanessa explained. "You should have it back. It's yours."

"But it's *not* mine," Mariko said. "It's Richelle's."

"Then Richelle should have it back."

"Richelle is dead."

"Oh! I'm so sorry."

"She passed about ten years ago now," Mariko Marsden explained. "Cancer. I heard through the grapevine."

Vanessa wondered if Mariko Marsden had cancer, too, if she was getting chemotherapy and that's why her eyebrows and eyelashes had fallen out. But it would probably be rude to ask, so she didn't. Instead she looked at the painting. The figure in the orange dress seemed very much like she could be a young Mariko Marsden. So Vanessa pointed to the other figure, the darker-skinned one with the Afro. "Was that her?"

"That was her."

"What was she like?"

"Richelle?" Mariko's tight-lipped expression relaxed, for a moment, into a smile as she studied the young woman in her painting. "She was whip smart. Pragmatic. Efficient. She had her entire life mapped out, which fascinated me. I remember I showed up here, let's see, it must have been the summer I was twenty. I was so young and I had no idea what I was doing. I'd dropped out of college and was hitchhiking around the country. Just going wherever the winds took me, which was the exact *opposite* of her. She had a six-month plan, a five-year plan, a twenty-year plan. Some truck driver dropped me off in Edgewood Falls. I

thought I'd only be here for a few days, but then I met Richelle, so I stayed."

"How long were you here for?" Vanessa asked. It was cool that such a famous artist had once lived right here, in her town. Why didn't anyone talk about that? Had her mom's news station ever done a story about it?

"About four months."

That wasn't long at all. No wonder Vanessa had never heard about Mariko living here. She barely had.

"Why only four months?"

"Four months was a long time for me! I was ready to move on."

"Why?" Vanessa asked again.

"I suppose I knew there was other stuff out there in the world, and I wanted to go experience it."

"What kind of other stuff?"

"Everything that wasn't right here." Mariko's face was stern again. "You know, you're asking a lot of questions about the details of what I was thinking a very, very long time ago."

"But what about Richelle?"

"What *about* Richelle?" Mariko Marsden asked back.

"When you left, did she go with you?"

Mariko Marsden laughed, as though the idea was ridiculous. "No. I told her she could come, but I knew she'd never consider it. Roaming the world for some indeterminate length of time was definitely *not* part of her twenty-year plan."

"Okay, so then what happened?" Vanessa asked.

"What do you mean, 'then what happened'? The entire rest of my life happened. And hers, too, I assume."

"You *assume*? You don't know?"

Mariko Marsden shrugged gracefully. "It was harder to keep in touch back in those days. No email, no 'DMing,' if that's what you call it. Long-distance phone calls cost money, and I was a broke artist. When someone's address or phone number changed, it could be hard to track them down again."

"But she was your *friend*," Vanessa reminded her.

"She was. And we had a fabulous summer together. The best! But as time went on, life took us in different directions, and we had less and less in common. Less and less to talk about. *C'est la vie*."

"Say la vee?" Vanessa repeated.

"It's French. It means *that's life*."

But *why*? *Why* was that life? And even if it *was*, why would anyone just accept it?

"You left her," Vanessa whispered.

"I left," Mariko Marsden said, twisting the plastic band tight around her index finger. "Leaving *her* wasn't the goal. It was just what happened. I had to go."

"No, you didn't," Vanessa said. She couldn't believe she was talking back to a grown-up, let alone a *famous* grown-up. But her righteous indignation on behalf of Richelle, on behalf of all those who got left behind, was too much to bear. It bubbled up inside and came spilling out. "You didn't have to go. You *chose* to go."

Mariko Marsden paused, like she'd never quite thought of it that way, and then nodded. "I do not have to defend to you, a child, the choices that I made fifty years ago."

That's because they're indefensible, Vanessa thought.

Vanessa had imagined maybe she'd return the painting to Richelle. Or maybe she'd return it to Maria. And that was what would happen, she supposed. Maria—Mariko Marsden—she would take it.

But she didn't deserve it.

It had nothing to do with Vanessa anymore, though. It did, for a while. But now it didn't.

After some time, Vanessa murmured a goodbye and quietly exited her museum. The artist stayed behind, staring at her own work, the plastic band twirling around and around in her hands.

CHAPTER 25

Vanessa stirred her soggy cereal around the bowl the following morning. Everything was out of her control, and she hated it. She couldn't save her father, or save her friendship with Bailey, or save the museum. She'd thought she could save Maria's painting, that could be the *one thing* she set right. But she couldn't even do that.

"So what's the plan?" Sterling asked. He was sitting next to her at the breakfast counter, and he spoke quietly, as their mother was on her computer in the next room.

Vanessa shrugged wearily. "I guess she'll take the painting. And then in a couple weeks they'll tear down the museum. And that'll be that. Like none of it was ever there at all. *C'est la vie.*"

"That stinks," Sterling said, pushing away his own cereal bowl.

"Yup."

"I *need* the museum," Sterling went on.

Vanessa needed it, too. But before she could say as much, her brother kept talking.

"High school is . . ." Sterling paused and looked away, searching for the right words. "Hard."

Vanessa nodded, like she knew, which she didn't really, but she could imagine.

"Especially with Dad being . . . you know," he went on.

Gone, Vanessa filled in silently. *Dead? Missing. Better when he's far away. But not so far away that he can't ever come back.*

"It's just, like, high school is . . . really big, I guess? And a lot of the other kids there seem, I don't know, like, a lot older than me?"

"You're a freshman," Vanessa pointed out. "A lot of them *are* older than you."

"Yeah. But they really *act* like it." Sterling bit his lower lip. "Middle school's easier."

"Middle school's not always so easy, either," Vanessa reminded him.

"For me," he clarified. "Middle school was easier for

me. Or at least it seems easier now, when I think about it. Like, give me middle school problems any day. So sometimes it's nice to kind of . . . pretend like I'm still a little kid. You know?"

Vanessa understood then. Her brother was trying to answer the question she'd asked him about why he spent so much time at the museum when, by all rights, he should have been beyond it. There was a new life ready for him, with older kids doing older-kid things. And he didn't want that life yet. Or maybe he did, a little, sometimes—but he still wanted his old life, too. And that's what the museum was for him. A way to be a kid for a little while longer.

Vanessa felt a surge of fondness for her brother. But aloud, all she said was, "Hey, who are you calling little?"

Her brother grinned and shoved her. "You, twerp."

Vanessa shoved him back.

"I'm sorry Mariko Marsden turned out to be such a disappointment," Sterling said.

"Oh, so you heard about this?" their mother asked, bustling into the kitchen.

Both kids stiffened. "Heard about what?"

Their mom removed her glasses to look at them. "I thought you just said something about Mariko Marsden.

The artist, you know? Am I hearing things? Anyway, it turns out she's in town! Literally *here*, in Edgewood Falls!"

Vanessa and Sterling exchanged a furrowed-brow look.

"That's . . . cool?" Vanessa said.

"It is!" their mother agreed cheerily. "You know that old falling-apart building near the park? Well, everyone thought it was empty, but somehow a Mariko Marsden painting wound up just sitting there, and nobody even knew! Can you believe it?"

Vanessa and Sterling shared a stunned silence.

"I was just as surprised as you," their mother told them. "I guess someone found it as they were prepping the building for demolition, and now Mariko Marsden has flown into town to see it. Everyone thought it was lost. I don't know if you kids have any sense of how accomplished an artist she is, but to somehow *find* a work of hers is—well, it's amazingly rare and very exciting."

"Very exciting," Sterling echoed, giving Vanessa a *HELP!* look.

"The station is doing a segment on it, so I thought I'd head over there to see the action for myself. How do you like this for a moral: Before you knock down a building, make sure you look inside!"

"The station," Vanessa repeated. "*Your* station? Your news station? Is going to film a story on this painting?"

"That's right!" Their mother beamed. "You see, the news is happening all the time, everywhere, even right in our own backyard. You should come with me, see it for yourself."

"Excuse us," Sterling said in a strangled voice. "We're going to . . . play outside."

He grabbed Vanessa's arm and pulled her out of the house. "What do we do?" he asked, breathing fast. "What do we do, what do we do, *what do we do?* When Mom or her coworkers look around the museum, they're going to see our exhibits, and she's going to *know* they're ours, and—"

"We're going to be in *so much trouble*," Vanessa finished.

"Can we pretend like it's not our stuff? Just, you know, fully lie to her?"

"The signs and maps are all in my handwriting," Vanessa reminded him. "The baseball card collection is obviously *your* baseball card collection. She'd never believe us."

Sterling buried his face in his hands.

"We need to beat the news crew to the museum," Vanessa responded. "We need to clear out everything. *Now.*"

There was no further discussion. The two kids bolted down the street, faster than they'd ever gone before, even faster than Vanessa had run the night of the burglary. Sterling pulled out his phone and called their friends as his feet pounded the pavement. "Museum!" he gasped into the phone. "Emergency! Move!"

The cul-de-sac was as empty as usual when they got there. No news crew, yet. They still had time. But how much?

Sterling leapt through the open window with such recklessness that the garbage bag curtain fell down. Before it could even hit the ground, Vanessa grabbed it. She started stuffing items inside of it, without any rhyme or reason, just whatever she could get her hands on. Einstein's squeaky football. Rosalie's batteries. Her jewelry box where they collected admission fees.

"I can't believe her," Vanessa fumed. "I can't *believe* her!"

"Mariko Marsden?" Eli asked, climbing into the museum breathlessly.

"Yes, Mariko Marsden!" Vanessa shouted. "*I* tracked her down. *I* told her where her painting was. *I* showed

her around the museum. I told her that grown-ups aren't allowed here, but that I would make an exception for her! *Just* for her! Because I thought that she, out of anyone, would *understand*! And then what does she do?"

Eli grabbed another garbage bag and started tossing his Einstein artifacts inside of it. The half-chewed bone. The threadbare bandana. The vet reports. All of it, once again, trash.

"She calls a *press conference*!" Vanessa answered her own question. "'Oh, hey, everyone, come on down to this secret museum, I have a bunch of kids I'd love to get in trouble!'"

Minutes later, Rosalie and Honore tumbled into the museum. "There's a car out there," Rosalie gasped out.

"Is it a news van?" Sterling asked.

"No. I don't think so. It looked like an ordinary car."

"It might be the producer," Vanessa said. "Hurry!" She knotted up the first full garbage bag and tossed it into the darkened far corner of one of the side rooms.

Honore ran all around, picking up the battery-powered lanterns and throwing them into a bag. Rosalie ripped down labels and pulled Honore's watercolors off the wall.

"Careful with those!" Honore exclaimed. "I worked very hard on them."

"We don't have time to be careful right now, Honore!" Rosalie shouted.

Eli peered through a gap in one of the boarded-up front windows. "Someone else just got here," he reported. "They're walking toward the museum . . ."

Honore gasped.

"Okay, no, wait, now they've stopped in the middle of the park and they're looking at their phone."

"If our parents find out that we've been hanging out in here . . ." Honore began.

"We'll be *dead*," Rosalie finished.

Vanessa's heart was pounding at what felt like a million beats per minute. There was no way they could clear out this entire museum, weeks of work and care and focus, in a matter of minutes. No way.

Yet somehow . . .

With all of them working together, no distractions, no directions, no need for conversation, just one single, unifying goal and a threat that was coming for them all . . .

They did.

Sterling dumped the final bag of their belongings into an unlit side room, and they scanned for anything they'd overlooked. The main room now was almost exactly as Vanessa had found it that day in March. Less dust, less

debris, fewer dead leaves—but nobody would notice that. And if they did, no one would think to credit the relative cleanliness to a group of kids. There was really only one object of note in the whole room now. Maria's painting, leaning against the wall, the center of attention.

"Let's get out of here," Sterling said, but as Vanessa stared at the canvas, she was struck by a sudden thought:

She could destroy it.

It would be so easy. She could punch a hole through it. Tear it up. Grab a marker and scribble all over it. She recalled what she'd thought when that klutzy museum guest had tripped into an exhibit, weeks ago: Beautiful things took a long time to make, but to ruin them took almost no effort at all.

Vanessa had been fascinated by the painting from the moment she found it. She had never considered destroying it. It was one of a kind. It was lovely. And once it was gone, it would be impossible ever to bring it back, and that alone was reason enough to preserve it.

On the other hand, Mariko Marsden was a traitor. And so wasn't this exactly what she deserved?

"Vanessa!" Rosalie shouted from the window. She had one leg already outside, ready to run. "Come *on*!"

Vanessa took a step. Away from the window. Toward the painting.

"The news van is pulling up!" Sterling yelled. "We're out of time!"

It would take only a second to destroy it. Like knocking over a piece of pottery. Or tearing down a building. Or firing a single bullet. One second, and it would never be the same again.

Vanessa reached out her arm.

And her phone began to ring.

"Not now!" Eli said.

"Leave it!" Honore said.

Vanessa pulled the phone out of her pocket, and she saw the name on the screen. He always did have the worst timing.

She answered.

"Daddy," Vanessa said.

"Vanessa," said her father. "It's me. I'm safe."

CHAPTER 26

Vanessa was in the park outside the museum now, still holding her phone, even though she had hung up already.

Sterling put his arm around her for a brief moment. "Dad's okay," he repeated, over and over. "Dad's okay." Vanessa, meanwhile, couldn't say anything at all.

Her father was fine. He was safe. He loved her.

Everything was good again.

Nearby, the news crew was setting up. There was a camera operator and a lighting person and a person with a microphone and a producer and a production assistant and an on-air personality, but none of them were paying any attention to Vanessa or her friends. They were just kids, after all, hanging out in a park.

Mariko Marsden climbed out of a car. Today she was dressed in brightly colored leggings and a cape. All the people from the local news station rushed up to her, but she marched right past them. She didn't slow down until she had reached Vanessa.

"I'm sorry," Mariko Marsden said.

Vanessa blinked at her. She hadn't expected this. In her experience, grown-ups didn't apologize to kids that much. And Mariko Marsden didn't even seem like a particularly *nice* grown-up.

Sterling patted Vanessa awkwardly on her back and moved away, giving her and the artist a moment to speak privately.

"I realize it must seem like I asked these reporters to come here," Mariko Marsden went on. "I didn't. But I *am* responsible for them showing up."

"What?" Vanessa asked.

"After I saw you yesterday, I took lots of photos of *The Angel Opens His Mouth*, and I shared them with my agent. Next thing you know, he's talked to my publicist, and she's called the local press, and they're going to do a story about this amazing discovery. They're running it

whether I'm part of it or not. So I agreed to an interview. At least by speaking on camera, I can control the narrative a bit."

"Oh," said Vanessa, who wasn't totally clear on what an agent or a publicist did, and also did not want to ask.

"I swear that I did not tell anyone about your museum," Mariko Marsden said, twisting a band around her fingers. It was a different color from yesterday's: That one was purple and plastic, this one was metallic. "You told me that it was a secret. That it was not for adults. I want you to know that I respect that. I take that very seriously. Even if it doesn't much seem like it." She gestured toward the news crew behind her.

Vanessa didn't know how to feel. Thanks to Mariko Marsden's carelessness, they'd had to dismantle their entire museum in twenty minutes. They'd been robbed of their last couple weeks of the museum, their time to give it the proper goodbye that it deserved, that they all deserved.

On the other hand, Mariko Marsden hadn't *meant* to ruin it.

Vanessa was suddenly, deeply glad that she had not hurt the painting. She felt ashamed that she'd even had the instinct. Ruining something by accident and ruining something on purpose were two very different matters.

"Why did you tell your agent at all?" Vanessa asked.

"Because I was trying to figure out what to do," Mariko Marsden responded. "That's why you asked me to come here, isn't it? The painting can't just stay where it is. It needs to go *somewhere*."

"Aren't you going to take it with you?" Vanessa asked.

"I don't keep my old artwork," Mariko Marsden said.

"You don't?" Vanessa said. "Why not? Don't you like it?"

"I like knowing that it's out there," Mariko Marsden said. "I like being able to visit my pieces, sometimes, in museums occasionally, or in photographs. But to have the actual, physical pieces with me, as an ongoing part of my life? No. It would be like living with ghosts."

"Ghosts?" Vanessa echoed.

"You put some of yourself into everything that you create," the artist explained. "That painting of me and Richelle? That represents a moment in time. I painted the person who I was and the feelings that I had and the world that I saw. And, like I said, it's nice to be able to visit my past self. But I'm not her anymore.

"Seeing that painting yesterday, for the first time in fifty years . . . it made me nostalgic for everything that went into it," Mariko Marsden went on, pulling her metallic band into a straight line, then coiling it back

up. "For being young and having no responsibilities, for the desperate intensity of that friendship, for that park that's now a shopping plaza. It was a beautiful life, what I had. But I don't want it back. I want whatever life comes next."

And that seemed to Vanessa a very good thing to want.

"So then what are you going to do with the painting?" Vanessa asked.

"What do *you* think I should do with it?" Mariko Marsden asked back.

"I don't know . . ." Vanessa chewed on the cuticle of her ring finger. "It must be worth so much. What did your agent and publicist think?"

"Vanessa," the artist said. "You found it. You took care of it. You gave people the opportunity to see it again. I want to hear *your* advice."

"Well . . ." Vanessa looked past Mariko Marsden, toward her friends, who were far enough away that they couldn't overhear this conversation, but not so far that she couldn't make out the expressions of awe and confusion on their faces as they watched her speak with this iconic creator. "I think the painting should just go to someone who will care about it," she said at last. "And care about your friendship with Richelle."

“Yes,” said Mariko Marsden, staring at Vanessa intently. “I think it should, too.”

“Ms. Marsden?” The production assistant approached her. “They’re ready for you.”

And Mariko Marsden turned away from Vanessa and headed toward the news crew.

Vanessa rejoined her friends. “What did she *say*?” Honore demanded, practically vibrating with excitement.

“She said she was sorry.” Vanessa stared across the park at Mariko Marsden, now speaking with a camera operator.

“Did she say anything about my watercolors, though?” Honore prodded. “Like, did she say, ‘Whoever painted those shows a lot of potential. I bet they’re going to be a professional artist someday?’”

“Um,” Vanessa replied. “Those weren’t her *exact* words . . .”

“There you are!” Vanessa and Sterling startled at the sound of their mother’s voice behind them.

“Hi, Mom,” Sterling said.

“Hi,” Vanessa echoed, trying to look as innocent as possible.

“I just got off the phone with your father,” their mom said, gathering them both in for a hug. “He said he already talked to you.”

Vanessa nodded. "He said they had trouble locating the next of kin for one of the soldiers, so the comm blackout dragged on for way longer than it should have, *and* the power was knocked out. But he's totally fine. Everyone in his unit is fine." She looked up at her mom. "He sounded really good."

"He sounded great," Mom agreed. She squeezed the kids' shoulders and stepped back. "And isn't this wonderful? A beautiful spring day, a world-famous artist, my newsroom breaking the story. *And* your father is safe and sound. What could be better?" She smiled at Honore, Rosalie, and Eli. "Hey, kids. I'm glad you all wanted to come down here to see it for yourself. How often do you get to see a real live news story play out before your very eyes? Now *this* will be something you can talk about at show-and-tell."

"We don't have show-and-tell anymore," Sterling said.

"We haven't had it since like third grade," Vanessa agreed.

"Well, you should show-and-tell people about this anyway," their mom said. "Come on, let's get a little closer so we can hear what she's saying."

They headed across the park until they were standing in the cul-de-sac just in front of the museum, behind the camera operator. Vanessa's mom gave little waves to all her coworkers.

"Mariko, we'll just record you walking through the museum, talking to us about the painting, how it was discovered, all that stuff," the producer said. "We'll edit it down back at the studio, so this can just be casual and natural, got it?"

Mariko Marsden glared at the producer, as if to communicate that she had never in her life been casual *or* natural.

"We're rolling," said the camera operator.

"I'm Rob Nelson, and I'm here today with the contemporary artist Mariko Marsden," said the on-air personality, a tanned man in a collared shirt. "You can see her work at the Museum of Modern Art in New York City, the Centre Pompidou in Paris, the Getty in Los Angeles, and in other top museums and galleries around the world. And a recent discovery means that you also could have seen her work right here, in Edgewood Falls, Ohio."

Rob turned to Mariko. "So how did you find out that a painting of yours—one of your earliest preserved paintings, if I'm not mistaken—had been sitting here in this decommissioned local museum?"

"I received an anonymous tip," Mariko Marsden responded. "So I flew out here to confirm that it was true."

"Any idea where that anonymous tip might have come from?" Rob asked.

Mariko's eyes flickered briefly past the camera operator, to Vanessa. "No," she said.

"Remarkable," said Rob. To the camera, he said, "This little building had served as a local museum for decades, but nearly twenty years ago, the town stopped funding it. Without a budget to maintain it, the collection was dismantled, with some of its pieces and archives going to the local library and town hall, others being auctioned off to private collectors, and some, unfortunately, being lost forever."

So Vanessa's collection *wasn't* the first to be removed from a museum, broken down, and redistributed. That same thing had happened before, right in this very building.

"How do you think your painting wound up left behind here?" the man asked Mariko Marsden.

"I have no idea," she answered. "I gifted the painting to a friend of mine, a woman who lived here in Edgewood Falls, in 1970. Until now, I had never been back here. Maybe she donated it to the museum at some point while the museum was still operational. She was a generous person; I could see her doing that. Or maybe she was angry with me and just wanted the painting out of her house."

Rob laughed at that. Mariko Marsden did not.

"I can't imagine she wouldn't have wanted to hold on to an original Mariko Marsden," Rob said. "What do you think it's worth?"

"That's a tasteless question, don't you think?" the artist responded.

Rob stopped laughing. "Well." He cleared his throat. "Let's go inside to see this miracle painting for ourselves, shall we?"

Mariko Marsden led the way through the window, followed by the camera operator, the on-air personality, the producer, and the whole rest of the team. Vanessa's mom went after them, and Vanessa went after her, but her mom held up an arm to stop her.

"I don't want you kids coming inside," she said.

Vanessa and her friends all looked at her mom, baffled.

"It might be dangerous," her mother explained. "This is an abandoned building. There could be broken glass, exposed nails, asbestos, faulty wiring—we don't know. It's not a place for kids."

Vanessa bit her cheek to keep from laughing. She could see Eli's mouth opening and closing, like he wanted *so badly* to talk back and was doing everything he could to keep it in.

"Mom, I think it's fine in there." Vanessa tried moving past her mom's outstretched arm, but she held firm.

"Vanessa, there are probably spiders in there," her mother said.

"I don't mind spiders *that* much," Vanessa said.

"Stay," their mother ordered, and she followed the rest of the crew inside.

And that, more than anything, made Vanessa realize: The museum did not belong to her anymore.

Left on their own outdoors, the kids looked at one another. "Let's just hope they don't go into any of the side rooms and start opening up trash bags," Rosalie said.

Vanessa craned her neck, but it was impossible to make out what was happening inside the building. The same privacy that had allowed them to run a secret museum was now working against them.

Had they left anything inside that would get them in trouble? They'd been in such a rush that she couldn't be certain. Had they left a label hanging on the wall? Had they forgotten an artifact in a display case?

If they had, it was too late to do anything about it.

So they stayed outside, and they waited. Eli sat down on the grass. Honore hopped up and down in little circles.

Vanessa dug in her fingernails to tear off a scab on the back of her hand.

A few minutes later, the news crew exited through the window. Eli bolted to his feet, and the kids all held their breath. But none of the adults paid them any attention. They walked right past them.

"What happened in there?" Vanessa whispered to her mom, trying not to seem so curious that it was suspicious.

"We saw the painting," her mom whispered back. "It's huge! I took a photo to show you because they're going to remove it for safekeeping right after the interview's finished. It's a good thing you didn't come in there, though. It's very dusty." She blew her nose into a tissue, as if to prove the point.

Vanessa almost collapsed with relief. They didn't know. The secret was safe.

Back in front of the museum, the interview with Mariko Marsden continued. "This building is due to be demolished in just a few weeks. So what's your plan for *The Angel Opens His Mouth and Speaks the Truth*?" the newscaster asked.

"I'm glad you asked," Mariko Marsden said. "I do have an idea, something I'm excited about. This is a very special old building. Once it's gone, it's gone forever, and that just

won't do. I'd like to endow this museum so it can reopen to the public."

Vanessa's mom gave a little gasp.

"What is she saying?" Vanessa whispered. "What does 'endow' mean?"

"It means that she wants to fund the museum," her mom whispered back. "With her own money."

Vanessa stared at the artist, openmouthed.

"So you're telling us," the reporter said, "that you plan to pay for this building to be brought back up to code? And you're going to rebuild the collection, and hire staff, and—"

"Yes," said Mariko Marsden. "Well, I don't want that much day-to-day involvement, but yes, I'll finance it all." She let out a little snort of laughter. "This interview is the first my business manager is hearing about this plan, so I'm sure he will have some questions as well! Look, I just had this idea, so I haven't worked out the details yet. That will be someone else's job. For my part, I have just three requirements."

Everyone was silent, listening.

"One, this building will once more serve as a museum open to the public, as it was intended to be. Two, my painting *The Angel Opens His Mouth and Speaks the Truth* will be permanently on display here. And three . . ." Mariko

Marsden again caught Vanessa's eye. "One section of the museum will be always and forever set aside for the children of Edgewood Falls to curate their own exhibitions."

"And how do you—" the newscaster began, but the artist cut him off.

"No further questions," she said. And she swished her cape around her and marched off to a waiting town car.

CHAPTER 27

That evening, they ordered in a feast of takeout Thai food: pad thai and pad see-ew and curries and Vanessa's favorite, Thai iced tea. It was a lot of food, but they had a lot to celebrate. Even more than Vanessa's mom knew.

"I *love* this idea of giving local kids a section of the museum to curate," she said, squeezing hot sauce over her rice and tofu. "I wonder how they'll decide who can get involved. Do you think you'd be interested in trying to do an exhibition there, once it reopens to the public?"

Sterling and Vanessa exchanged a quick look across the dinner table.

"Maybe," Vanessa said. "I'm glad that they're doing that. I really am. But I don't know how much I want to be part of it. It'll still be, like, an official museum run by grown-ups. I bet it'll have glossy floors and glass windows and electricity and even bathrooms."

"Yes," agreed her mother with a laugh. "We can be pretty sure that it will have all those things."

"And that's good," Vanessa said. "It *should* have those things. It'll just be different, that's all."

"Different from what?" her mom asked.

"Different from how I would run a museum if it was all mine, I guess." Vanessa took a big bite of noodles. In some regards, this new museum would be better than hers. They'd probably have a real security system, for example, so thieves couldn't just come in and help themselves to the exhibits. It could still be good. But it would be good in a new way.

"Sterling?" their mom said. "Would you want to curate an exhibition when the museum opens? Oh, I have an idea—you could display that baseball card collection of yours!"

Sterling spent a little too long wiping his mouth, like he was trying to keep his mom from seeing his face. Finally,

he put down his napkin and said, "I don't think so. Like Vanessa said, it's really cool that they're doing this. And I bet a lot of kids are going to be into it. But me? I think I'll be too old for it."

Vanessa gave her brother a tiny smile across the table. He smiled back.

"What?" their mom asked.

"What what?" Vanessa replied.

"You're grinning at each other. What's that about? Are you in cahoots on something?"

"What's cahoots?" asked Vanessa.

"We smile at each other all the time," said Sterling. "You know. 'Cause we love each other."

"Yeah, right." Their mom rolled her eyes.

"Would you rather we fight with each other?" Sterling asked. "We can fight."

"We can totally fight," Vanessa agreed. "Would that be better, Mom?"

She held up her hands in defeat. "You know what? Smile all you want. I'm not going to ask any more questions."

On command, Sterling smiled widely, his mouth full of half-chewed food.

"Grooooossss," Vanessa moaned.

"Oh, that reminds me," their mom said, "if you come across an old piano outside, do *not* get too close."

"Why does that remind you of . . . Actually, never mind," said Sterling, swallowing his food at last. "I don't even want to know."

"So what did you two think of Mariko Marsden?" their mom asked. "You know she's probably the most famous person you've ever been that close to. That doesn't happen every day."

"She wasn't as bad as she seemed," said Vanessa.

"She was kinda weird," Sterling said.

"Maybe a little eccentric," their mom allowed. "Plenty of artists are eccentric."

"How come she didn't have any eyebrows or eyelashes?" Sterling asked. "Her face looked funny with those eyebrow lines painted on."

"I was actually wondering about that myself," their mom said. "I thought she might have some kind of condition that causes hair loss. Nadine—you know, the producer there today—told me that Mariko Marsden has something called trichotillomania."

"Tricho-what?" Vanessa asked.

"That's what I asked. *Trichotillomania* is apparently a psychological condition that causes people to pull out

their own hair. Nadine hadn't heard of it, either, before she started doing her prep for today's interview."

Vanessa caught her breath. She felt like a puzzle piece she hadn't even been looking for had suddenly clicked into place.

"Why would anyone pull out their own hair?" Sterling asked with a shudder. "Doesn't that hurt?"

"I'm sure it does," their mom said.

Vanessa didn't have to wonder if it hurt. She knew that it did. Not a lot, and not all the time, but a little. That wasn't why you'd do it, though. The hurt was an accident, a by-product. The pulling was the point.

"I don't know any more about it than you do," their mom said. "Why don't you go look it up?"

And so after dinner, that's what Vanessa did. She sat down on the living room couch and typed *trichotillomania* into the search bar.

Hundreds of results came up. Maybe thousands. Had everybody except her already known about this?

She started reading:

> Trichotillomania, often referred to as simply trich (pronounced like "trick") is part of a family of psychological conditions called body-focused repetitive behaviors, or BFRBs.

"BFRB," Vanessa whispered as quietly as she could, trying out how the letters felt on her tongue.

> BFRBs can take many forms, including hair-pulling (trichotillomania), skin-picking (excoriation disorder), nail-biting, cheek and lip-chewing, and more. Their effects can range from the minor (e.g., impermanent skin scarring) to the extreme (e.g., pulling out hair to the point of complete baldness, or picking skin to the point of serious infection). What all BFRBs have in common is that they are compulsive, uncontrollable self-grooming and self-soothing behaviors that happen without the sufferer's choice.

Vanessa's eyes were wide, unblinking. Was this article about *her*?

Surely not. Because she could stop picking her skin at any time, if she really wanted to. If she really, *really* tried.

But was that true? If she *could* stop . . . then wouldn't she have done it already?

Was she like Mariko Marsden?

> Psychologists estimate that between two and five percent of the population suffers from some sort of BFRB.

Two to five percent?! There were two hundred students in Vanessa's grade. If these psychologists were right, then there were at *least* four kids just in her grade at Edgewood Falls Middle School who had this condition. Why had she never noticed this before? Had she ever seen anyone else pulling out their hair, or picking at their skin, like her?

> Because BFRBs often go unreported, the actual number may in fact be even higher. Many sufferers experience shame and embarrassment around their conditions, and therefore they do not talk about them. They mistakenly believe that BFRBs are their own fault. This perspective assumes that picking is a conscious choice that the individual is making, and that they are free to choose otherwise. For people with BFRBs, this is not in fact the case. Any BFRB sufferer who has tried using willpower, rules, or shame to stop picking can attest that such approaches do not work.

Vanessa looked down at her leg, curled up under her on the couch. While she'd been reading this article, she had torn off a blister on the sole of her foot, exposing the soft, raw skin underneath. It would be uncomfortable to walk on it now, Vanessa knew.

Was it really possible that this wasn't her fault? That it *wasn't* because she was weak or broken or gross? That it wasn't a bad choice that she made and kept making, but that it simply . . . was? Like the cleft palate she had been born with. It was just a part of her. There was no one to blame.

But if she hadn't caused it, then how could she fix it?

Similar to how a depressed person can't just "cheer up," an individual with ADHD can't just "pay attention," a person with an anxiety disorder can't just "stop worrying," a person with anorexia can't just "eat some food," and a person with a drug addiction can't just "stop using," it's crucial to understand that a person with a BFRB can't just "stop picking."

Research into effective treatment for BFRBs is ongoing. No truly successful medication has yet been found, but working with a therapist trained in treating BFRBs can often have a beneficial impact. However, even with therapeutic treatment, recovery—if it happens—can often take years.

Many people with BFRBs find that they can sometimes offset the urge to pick by keeping their hands

busy with fidgets. While this doesn't stop the picking behavior, it redirects it to items outside of the person's own body.

Fidgets! *That's* what Mariko Marsden's little bands must have been. And maybe Vanessa's origami was a sort of fidget, too. She just hadn't known it.

There was a lot she hadn't known.

Vanessa set down her phone. She looked instead at her hands, scarred and chewed and flaking and mottled. Inside her was a whole mix of conflicting emotions, like cookie dough ingredients that hadn't been stirred together.

There *was* something different about her.

But it *wasn't* her fault.

And she *wasn't* the only one.

And it *could* be fixed.

But fixing it would be *hard*—maybe impossible—and take ages, if it ever happened at all.

She didn't know what to do with all these new pieces of information, how to stir them together into something palatable. For now, there was no responding, no fixing, no next steps. There was just knowing. Just sitting in her skin, ragged as it was, and being.

CHAPTER 28

As spring faded into summer, construction began on the museum. Bulldozers and cranes surrounded it. Mariko Marsden's painting was brought to town hall for safekeeping for the time being, and then the museum's interior was gutted. Construction workers figured out how to install a brand-new floor. Electricians came and figured out how to rewire the building for lights. Plumbers came and figured out how to fix the bathrooms. Professional restorers came with tall machines and cleaned the design at the top of the rotunda. Vanessa watched it all from the street. The city didn't have an estimated reopening date for the museum yet, but the newspaper said the construction shouldn't take more than a year.

A year was a long time. In the meantime, life went on. Summer break began. Vanessa kept making her origami. Rosalie kept doing her science projects. Eli taught Tesla how to lie down and roll over. And invitations started to arrive.

The first was from Chloe, Vanessa's classmate who had been among the earliest to visit the museum. "Do you want to visit my museum?" Chloe asked Vanessa. "It's not in a real museum building. It's just in my garage."

It still felt like a museum, though. Chloe collected snow globes from all over the world, and she had organized them geographically, along with labels providing information about the countries they came from. She had a whole shelf in her garage just for displaying them.

The girl who had knocked over Bailey's pottery started a museum, too. Hers was a horse museum, in her basement. "I've never ridden a horse," she confessed to Vanessa and Rosalie, when they came to visit, "but I'm obsessed with them." Her exhibition included images cut out from a horse wall calendar, horse figurines, a single stirrup, and even an old TV playing horse videos.

Soon, it seemed like museums were popping up everywhere in Edgewood Falls—in bedrooms and kitchens and backyards—and with every sort of exhibition—soccer and the Salem Witch Trials and old T-shirts.

Vanessa had started something more than a single museum. She had started a movement.

And then, one day in July, Vanessa received an invitation that she had never expected, to a museum she couldn't have imagined.

Do you want to come over and see my museum? Bailey messaged.

Vanessa didn't reply right away. She didn't know what to say.

She went to the lake with Honore, Rosalie, and Eli. Not Sterling—he'd gotten a summer job as a counselor-in-training at a local day camp, and now even when he wasn't working, he was hanging out with the other C.I.T.s. Some of them had come over to the house, but they didn't take any interest in Vanessa and they ate all the best snacks.

"I miss the museum," Honore said as she dangled her feet off the dock. They'd risked going back only once since Mariko Marsden made her pronouncement, a quick rescue mission for their garbage bags of stuff. The next time any of them returned, it would be as guests.

"At least we still have the artifacts to remember it by," Eli said.

"*I* don't," Vanessa reminded them.

"I don't need the artifacts to remember it," Rosalie said. "There's no way I'm ever going to forget our museum."

And Vanessa agreed.

Both the museum and Bailey would be part of Vanessa forever. Even if one day she didn't even think about them or miss them, like how Mariko Marsden felt about Richelle. Even then, they would still be some of the building blocks that made her who she was. She didn't need the artifacts to prove that all this had been real and had mattered. She, herself, was the proof.

"So what are we going to do next?" Eli asked.

"Diving board?" Vanessa suggested.

"No," Eli said. "I meant, like *next* next. Like instead of the museum."

"I wonder if we could find an abandoned amusement park," Rosalie said. "And start running our own rides and games and stuff."

"Or an abandoned ice cream factory," Honore suggested. "Imagine if we had our own ice cream brand. What should we call it?"

"Exactly how many abandoned businesses do you think there are in this town?" Vanessa asked, but already her mind was whirring with possibilities. "You know what could be cool? Setting up our own post office. Kids bring

us packages and letters and stuff, and we distribute them. We don't even need an abandoned post office to do that. We could just do it from my house. It wouldn't take much space. Unless the packages are really big."

"What about a zoo?" Eli asked. "Could we run a zoo?"

"We'd need animals," Honore said.

"Tesla is an animal. And you're an animal."

"Hey!" Honore objected.

"I'm just saying. Humans are animals. So that's two species already."

They kept brainstorming until the lifeguards made everyone head to shore. As they packed up, Vanessa said, "Hey—thanks for still wanting to do stuff together, even once the museum is gone."

"Obviously," said Eli. "It's not like we were hanging out with you just because you had a museum."

"Obviously," Vanessa agreed, but she couldn't stop a grin from spreading across her face. She hadn't known for sure. It was nice to hear someone say it.

Eli's parents came to pick him up, and a few minutes later Vanessa's mom pulled her car around. Vanessa laid down her towel on the passenger seat so she wouldn't drip all over it. She stared out the window, chewing on her lip as her mom drove away.

"How was the lake?" her mom asked.

Vanessa didn't bring up the dreams of a zoo or an ice cream parlor or a post office. Instead she said, "I got a text from Bailey."

"Oh?"

"She asked if I wanted to come over to see some stuff at her house."

"And do you want to?" Vanessa's mom asked.

"I don't know."

Her mom nodded and checked her rearview mirror. "That makes sense."

"Do you think I should?"

"I don't think there's a 'should' here," her mom said. "Either answer could be the right one. Sometimes what helps me decide what to do is imagining how I'd feel if I did it. Why don't you try that? How do you imagine you'd feel if agreed to go over there?"

"Scared," Vanessa answered immediately.

"And how do you imagine you'd feel if you told her no?"

Vanessa had to think about that one for a moment. Eventually, she said, "Sad."

Her mom nodded again. "And does that help you figure out what you want to do?"

"Yeah," Vanessa said. "It does, actually."

She hated being scared. But she would rather be scared than sad.

And with that in mind, she decided it was time to do something else scary.

"Mom?" Vanessa said quietly.

"Mm-hmm?"

Vanessa paused, letting the words sit on her tongue. Once it was said, it was out there. It would be real.

She could still say *never mind, it's nothing.* It wasn't too late.

She took a deep breath. "You remember Mariko Marsden?"

"Of course."

"You remember how you said she has that thing? Where she pulls out her hair?"

"Trichotillomania."

"Right. So . . . I think I have that, too. The thing that Mariko Marsden has."

Her mom shot her a quick glance before turning back to face the road. "I don't think so, honey. All your eyelashes and eyebrows are intact, as far as I can tell. Remember when you read the Babysitters Club for the first time and you thought you might have diabetes? You don't need to worry about coming down with every medical condition that you hear about."

"It's not my eyebrows," Vanessa said. "It's other stuff."

"What other stuff?" her mom asked.

Vanessa didn't want to say it. "I've been reading a bunch about it online. Can you read one of the articles I found about it?"

"Sure," her mom said. "Do you want to read it aloud to me?"

Vanessa shook her head.

"Then can it wait until we get home?"

"I really want you to read it now," Vanessa said.

And to her surprise, her mom turned into the nearest parking spot, put the car in park, and held out her hand. "I'm ready."

Vanessa pulled up one of the many articles that she'd read about BFRBs over the past few weeks. She chose one from a reputable source, a publication her mom had heard of, so she'd know that she could take it seriously, that this wasn't just one of those made-up internet things.

Her mom took the phone and bowed her face over it, reading silently. Vanessa waited, peeling off layer after layer of skin around her fingernails.

After a few minutes, her mom handed the phone back to her. "Okay," she said.

"Okay?" Vanessa repeated. Did her mom believe her? Was she mad? Or ashamed?

"I don't know anything about this condition," her mom said. "I don't know what causes it or how concerned I should be. But here's what I *do* know." She took Vanessa's hands in her own and stared intently into her eyes. "I know that I trust you, and I love you, and I respect you. We're going to learn about this together, and figure out a way to handle it together. And I'm going to be here to help you in any way that I can.

"That's all I know right now. But it's a lot more than I knew ten minutes ago. How does that sound?"

Vanessa nodded and grinned. "That sounds okay to me."

She felt like a weight had been lifted from her chest. She wasn't all better. She wasn't even a little bit better. But she wasn't alone anymore, either. And for now, that was good enough.

CHAPTER 29

When Vanessa got to Bailey's house, a week after she'd received her invitation, she paused for a moment on the stoop. She didn't know what to expect. Would Bailey's new friends be here, too? Was this an opportunity for Bailey to apologize, or to find a new way to make her feel bad, or to pretend like nothing had happened? She pulled out a brand-new fidget, just like Mariko Marsden's, so she'd have something to do with her hands.

Since Vanessa had told her mom about her BFRB, not much had changed. Her mother had asked if Vanessa wanted to tell her dad, too, and Vanessa said that it was okay if her father knew about it, but that she didn't want to be the one to tell him.

So her mom and dad had a call that Vanessa didn't have to be part of, and since then her dad had been sending over links with information about therapists at the VA hospital. When Vanessa didn't respond right away, he added that he would even pay out-of-pocket for her to see a private psychologist, someone who wasn't part of the military's healthcare system, if she wanted. "Anything for my baby," he said.

He wasn't telling her that she *had* to go see a therapist . . . but he was definitely implying that she *should*. Her mom said that it was up to her, and she wasn't sure yet. She was thinking about it.

Her dad was always going to try to fix problems as soon as he heard about them. That's just who he was. He didn't like that this was a problem with no obvious solution. He might not have even been totally convinced that Vanessa couldn't simply stop picking on her own if she just worked harder. But Vanessa knew that he was at least *trying* to understand it, and that was something.

She hadn't told anybody else yet. Not even her brother, not even Rosalie. Maybe someday she would.

Now, she wound her new fidget around her thumb and held her breath.

The door opened, and Bailey stood alone on the other side.

"Hi," said Vanessa.

"Hi." Bailey seemed nervous, too. She was knotting her fingers together and shifting her weight from foot to foot. "My museum is upstairs."

Vanessa followed her to the upstairs hallway, where they had once spent so much of their lives playing together. The site of that infamous fashion show. Now, it had exhibits laid out against the wall, going from one end of the corridor to the other.

Vanessa took a look at the displayed items, and she immediately knew where they had come from. Fury came coursing through her veins.

"I *knew* you were the thief," she said to Bailey. "I knew it! You acted like I was crazy and told me I was accusing you for no reason, and that whole time you had everything from my museum right here in your house."

"I didn't," Bailey insisted.

"Bailey! The proof is *right here*. You invited me over to see it!"

Bailey exhaled a long breath, blowing her bangs out of her eyes. "I didn't steal any of this. Lisa took it. I had no idea. I just found out last week."

"Oh." Vanessa sank down onto the carpet, her rage gone as quickly as it had come. Bailey joined her. "Why? Why would she do that?"

"I'm not sure," Bailey answered. "I was over at her house last weekend, and I saw the guinea pig place mat on her kitchen table."

"What?" Vanessa was indignant. "That's *your* place mat."

"I know! I asked where she'd gotten it from, and she was all mysterious and then eventually was like, 'I rescued it for you.'"

"*Rescued* it?" Vanessa repeated. "From what? I wasn't, like, keeping it a prisoner."

"Lisa thought you were. Her friend Astrid went to the museum and told Lisa that there was this whole exhibition about what a terrible person I was."

Vanessa reddened. "I didn't—"

"So Lisa decided to go to the museum to scope it out for herself. And she decided that Astrid was right, and the exhibition made me look bad, so she took it all down so that nobody else would go and see what you said about me."

"She stole from me," Vanessa said.

"She swears she was just trying to protect me," Bailey said.

Vanessa doubted that Lisa's motivations were as pure as she claimed. More likely, Lisa hated seeing evidence of Vanessa's years of friendship with Bailey, when she, Lisa, had only known Bailey for a few months. Or maybe Lisa simply wanted to do something mean to Vanessa just because she could. Sometimes people didn't need any more reason than that.

But Vanessa also imagined for a moment what *she* would do if she saw something that seemed like it might hurt Bailey. She liked to think she would handle it in a calm, reasonable way. But maybe she wouldn't. Maybe she, too, would steal and lie, if she thought that's what a good friend would do.

"Lisa can be really mean sometimes," Vanessa said at last.

"So can you," Bailey said.

Vanessa opened her mouth to protest, then closed it. She'd had a whole batch of labels at the museum that proved Bailey's point.

"I'm not defending her," Bailey added. "She *did* steal from you. And she didn't tell me what she was doing, because she knew I'd tell her not to. That's messed up."

Vanessa hoped that this would be the end of Bailey's friendship with Lisa. But Bailey didn't say

anything about that. Instead she said, "I'm sorry I never made it to your museum. Everyone who saw it said it was amazing."

"Thank you." Vanessa found her voice. "It was." *You could have been part of it*, she thought. *You could have been central to the whole thing. But you chose otherwise.* The thought made Vanessa sad—not for herself, but for Bailey. It was Bailey who missed out.

"Do you . . ." Bailey looked nervous again. "Do you want to look at *my* museum?"

"I've seen all these artifacts before," Vanessa reminded her. "You know, because they're actually mine."

"But you haven't seen how *I* display them," Bailey pointed out. Which was a good point. If there was one thing Vanessa had discovered from redoing her exhibition so many times, it's that how you interpreted an item mattered every bit as much as the item itself.

"You're right." Vanessa climbed to her feet.

"It's mostly chronological," Bailey said. "It starts at this end."

Which meant that it started, of course, with Gibby Giraffe.

ITEM #1: GIBBY GIRAFFE SLAP BRACELET

When Vanessa moved to town at the start of second grade, I really wanted to be friends with her. I had seen her before, when she came to Pancho's with her family. She seemed awesome, and I was so excited to discover that she was in my class. On our first day of school, I saw that she had a Gibby Giraffe stuffed animal. I didn't know much about Gibby Giraffe. I'd only seen that show once or twice. But I figured that if Vanessa liked it, then it must be good. I told her I was a Gibby Giraffe fan, too, and that's how we started talking. After that I watched as much Gibby Giraffe as I could find, and guess what? It was good.

Vanessa looked up from the exhibit. "I never knew that," she whispered. "You really weren't a *Gibby Giraffe* fan before you met me?"

Bailey shook her head.

"You didn't have to pretend to watch a TV show that you didn't," Vanessa told her. "I would have been your friend anyway."

"I didn't want to risk it," Bailey said.

Not all of the items in Bailey's museum held surprises. Some of them were almost word-for-word how Vanessa had presented them.

ITEM #6: THE DAYS ARE JUST PACKED: A CALVIN AND HOBBES COLLECTION, BY BILL WATTERSON

Vanessa and I both love this book! We like to quote lines from it to each other.

Other exhibits, however, had new labels that made Vanessa see them differently.

ITEM #15: TWO-HEADED MONSTER HALLOWEEN COSTUME

This costume was Vanessa's idea. She kept showing me all of her ideas for how to make it our best costume ever. I wasn't really into it but I didn't know how to tell her no without disappointing her. I wanted to do something cute, like bunnies, but she insisted that Halloween costumes were supposed to be scary and if we were bunnies we'd be doing it wrong. So I did what she wanted, but when I showed up to school

wearing my half of the monster costume, the very first person to see me—Kevin Donnelly—said, "Oh, whew, Bailey, I'm so glad you already knew."

And I said, "Knew what?"

And he said, "Knew that you're a disgusting hairy monster. I thought I was going to have to tell you, but fortunately you figured it out on your own."

I was so upset that I changed out of my costume before Vanessa even got to school. I didn't want to tell anyone what Kevin had said. So I just wore normal clothes all day and Vanessa was mad at me and it was the worst Halloween ever.

"Kevin really said that to you?" Vanessa was furious. "Why didn't you tell me? I would have punched him. Or, worse—I would have told on him! That's bullying!"

"I didn't want you to tell on him," Bailey said. "I just wanted to not feel like a hairy monster."

Vanessa had no memory of Bailey mentioning that she didn't want to be a two-headed monster for Halloween that year. She wondered if Bailey really had argued against it and Vanessa had just ignored it because she knew what she wanted to do. Or maybe Bailey *hadn't* actually said anything against the idea; maybe she'd just

quietly shown less enthusiasm than Vanessa and hoped that Vanessa might notice.

And she felt bad. Because Bailey had the worst Halloween ever, and she was part of the reason why—at the time, even glad for it, because she *wanted* Bailey to suffer for not wearing her half of the monster and costing them the prize at the school costume contest.

As Vanessa got down to the far end of the hallway, she came to some items that hadn't been in her museum. Items from Bailey's personal collection. And Vanessa didn't see what these items had to do with their friendship—until she started reading.

ITEM #19: GIRL SCOUTS ENTREPRENEURS BADGE

Vanessa really wanted us to join a Girl Scout troop. I didn't care either way, but Vanessa said that I had to, that the point wasn't for HER to be a Girl Scout, it was

for us BOTH to be Girl Scouts, together. So we joined, and it turned out to be the best! We earned badges and sang funny songs and got to ride horses and learn how to pitch a tent.

But after just a couple months, Vanessa decided she didn't feel like being a Girl Scout anymore. She said we should both quit. She said she knew us, and we weren't the Girl Scouting type.

So I quit. I still kinda miss it.

ITEM #20: HOSPITAL BRACELET

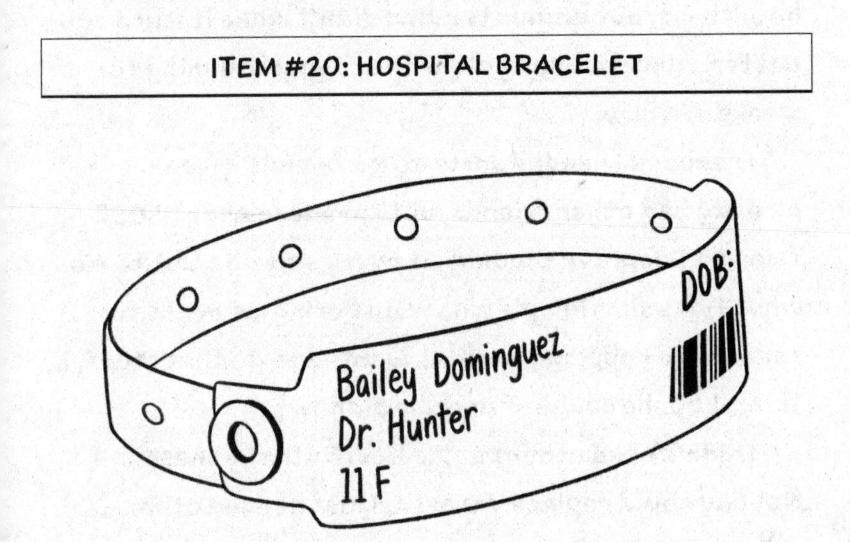

Last summer I got pneumonia and I had to stay in the hospital for a few nights. It was really scary. I felt like I couldn't breathe. And then I had to recuperate at home for weeks. And that wasn't scary, but it was extremely boring.

Throughout it all, I felt so alone. I had my family. But I didn't really have friends who were there for me. Vanessa knew that I was sick, but she was in Germany. She couldn't visit me, and she didn't even call me very often because there's a time difference and she was busy having fun European adventures with her dad. I totally understood why she couldn't be with me, but understanding didn't make it much better. I was still lying alone in bed and coughing for weeks in a row.

I realized I needed some other friends. I mean, I already had other friends, but I needed other CLOSE friends. People who would sit by my side and talk to me when I was sick. People who would bring me books to read in the hospital. Vanessa wanted to do that stuff, I think, but she couldn't and she didn't.

I didn't need other people INSTEAD of Vanessa. Nobody could replace Vanessa. I just needed other people AS WELL AS Vanessa. I had a whole life with Vanessa at the center of it, and last summer I realized that Vanessa couldn't always be there.

Vanessa realized she was crying as she finished reading the label. "I really *want* to always be there for you," she told Bailey, grabbing her hands. "I know that sometimes I'm not. I know that sometimes I show up late to your Christmas pageants or don't pay attention to what you want or leave the country while you're sick. I'm not trying to let you down. I *want* to always be at the center of your life."

"But that's not fair," Bailey said. "Because I'm not always at the center of *your* life."

"Are you mad at me?" Vanessa asked.

"I wasn't mad at you when I got sick and you weren't there. I just decided I would make more friends and do more things on my own, so I never felt that way again. But then you kept trying to stop me! And, yeah, *then* I got mad at you."

This led Vanessa to the most recent items in the display.

ITEM #21: PARTY INVITATION

I got invited to a slumber party at Kylie's. Vanessa was annoyed because she wasn't invited. She said I should hang out with her that night instead. When I went to the slumber party, Vanessa accused me of liking Kylie better than her. I felt like Vanessa didn't want me to have any other friends. Like she was basically saying, "You can be friends with me, or you can be friends with anybody else in the whole world, but you can't do both."

ITEM #22: MOVIE TICKET

I went with Lisa and Kylie to see Attack of the Killer Zombies. I asked Vanessa to join us, but she doesn't like scary movies, so she didn't come. She told me that I didn't like scary movies, either. She told me that they gave me nightmares. I said that used to be true, but I was older and braver now, and maybe I could handle those movies now. Vanessa told me that I was changing myself to try to fit in with the "popular kids" and that I was ignoring what "actually matters" to me to just go along with whatever they wanted.

I kept trying to get just a little distance from Vanessa, and every time, I discovered that there was no such thing. My choices were all Vanessa all the time—exactly the way we had always been—or no Vanessa at all. There was no in-between.

There was only one exhibit left, at the very end of the hallway. Vanessa crouched down to look at it.

ITEM #23: FRIENDSHIP BRACELET

"This one isn't in chronological order," Vanessa said, looking up at Bailey. "This is from fourth grade."

"Read the label, dummy."

ITEM #23: FRIENDSHIP BRACELET

I stitched this bracelet for Vanessa over spring break of fourth grade, while she was visiting her dad in Virginia. She wore it every day for almost a year until the knot unraveled.

Last week, I got the bracelet back. And I stitched it up again. I made it stronger and thicker this time. I added new colors and new designs. And I hope that sometimes, someday, Vanessa will wear it again.

Through her tears, Vanessa smiled at Bailey. Maybe, if they were lucky and if they tried hard, their friendship could be like her museum. It had been broken and decrepit, until eventually the whole thing had to be gutted. But it would be rebuilt and relaunched as something shiny and mostly unfamiliar. Different, but still there. Hers, but not only hers. Good in a new way.

Vanessa reached out her arms, and Bailey gave her a long hug. Vanessa tied the friendship bracelet around her wrist and held it up to the light. They both admired it.

"Do you want to stay for a while?" Bailey asked.

"I can't right now," Vanessa said. "I'm meeting up with my museum friends to work on our next project."

"Is it another museum?" Bailey asked.

"Nope. It's something brand-new. You'll see." Bailey walked Vanessa downstairs. At the door, Vanessa said, "Maybe we could hang out sometime later this week?"

"Yeah," Bailey said. "I'd like that." She closed the door behind Vanessa, and from opposite sides of the screen, they waved goodbye.

There's a place for what they were, Vanessa thought, as she headed off to find her new friends. That place was in a museum. And there would be a place for what they would become. She just didn't know what it would be yet.

ACKNOWLEDGMENTS

First and foremost, a massive thank you to my editor, Maggie Lehrman, for her patience and support as I found my way through this story. Thanks to Jacqueline Li for the evocative illustrations, and to Chelsea Hunter, Emily Daluga, Maggie Moore, Megan Carlson, Carrie Parker, Diane Aronson, Margo Winton Parodi, and the rest of the team at Abrams for making this beautiful book that you now hold in your hands. Thanks to my agent, Stephen Barbara, for his perspective and perseverance.

Thanks to Kirsten Madsen and Alexis Hyde for talking to me about museum curation. To AJ Boyes and Ian Kemp for advising me on military life. And to Priscilla Elliott for sharing her expertise on BFRBs.

A number of very good novels helped me figure out how to crack this one. I'd especially like to acknowledge the inspiration I gleaned from Zilpha Keatley Snyder's *The Egypt Game* and from E. L. Konigsburg's *From the Mixed-up Files of Mrs. Basil E. Frankweiler.*

I was also inspired by the many museums I've visited all over the world—the smaller and more niche, the better—including cat museums in Amsterdam and rural North Carolina, the bunny museum in Altadena, the salt and pepper shaker museum in Gatlinburg, the pencil museum in England's Lake District, the potato museum on Prince Edward Island, the playing card museum in Havana, et cetera, et cetera. Atlas Obscura has been a terrific resource in my ongoing search for unusual museums.

This is the first book I've ever published that Elyse Hughes won't immediately buy, attend the launch party for, and post about on social media. I really wish that weren't the case.

Thanks to Marit Weisenberg for the brainstorming sessions, and to Rebecca Serle for the writing sessions. To Emily Heddleson, my favorite and best museum-going partner in crime. To Brian Pennington for his belief in me. Kendra Levin, here's your abandoned ice cream factory book at last—I hope you like it.

Finally, as always, thank you to my parents. Your love makes everything possible.